ZEN, MISSISSIPPI

ZEN, MISSISSIPPI
M. David Hornbuckle

M. David Hornbuckle

ZEN, MISSISSIPPI

Tritone Media
New York, Birmingham

Published by
Tritone Media
Old Chelsea Station
P.O. Box 632
New York, NY 10113

Design by Marie Mundaca

Please visit the website at mdavidhornbuckle.com

Library of Congress Control Number: 2009943311

Zen, Mississippi
ISBN: 978-0-9849495-4-0

Printed in the USA
First Printing April 2010
e d c b

Acknowledgments

Thanks to everyone at Writer's Voice, where I workshopped much of this novel —especially Marcia, Grace, Karen, Kathleen, and Jim. I'd like to extend my greatest appreciation to my friends George and Janice, who read early drafts of this and told me it wasn't done yet.

ZEN, MISSISSIPPI

Prelude: 1987

Dobby takes a swallow of beer from a brown bottle, then sets it back on top of a wooden fence post. He resumes sweeping dry pine needles, steering them into neat piles with a pushbroom to form a crenelated wall around the edges of the driveway. After another and final swig of the beer, he tosses the bottle into a 44-gallon plastic trash can where it clinks against the dozen or so he consumed earlier in the afternoon and uncounted others that he emptied over the last few days.

The summer of '87 covers him in a hot white blanket of regret, drains him of damn nearly all his worth. He squints into the distance and sees the blonde girl Ashley, one of his son Patrick's classmates in the elementary school, approaching on a two-wheeler. He finds just enough mettle within himself to crack a weak joke as she comes within talking distance. "Better stay out of the sun, Ashley," he says with a yellowed grin. "Yer turnin' into a nigger."

Giggling, innocent, she passes. He follows to the edge of the street, watching until she disappears over the horizon. When he turns back around, his house is staring at him, a pocked goblin face. It's just because the symmetry of the two second-story windows and because the exterior paint is peeling off in verdigris chunks. Although he manages to keep the lawn meticulous, he's yet to get around to repainting outside or in, or to repairing the rotten boards near the edge of the porch, or to replacing that section of roof that leaks during heavy rains. Keeping up the lawn seems to be about as much as he can handle. Gives him something to do during the day on weekends.

The house is one his parents had owned—perhaps built, he's not sure—though it's not the one he grew up in; that one was on the other side of the highway, and his parents sold it when they retired. This place had been abandoned for a couple of years after his mama died, his daddy having died a few years before that. Dobby moved in when Sally kicked him out last spring. There wasn't much else available in Lyonness at the time, and he didn't have much money. If he hadn't had this house to move into, he might have had to relocate to Northport or Columbus, or even as far as Birmingham of Memphis for chrissake, take another job doing godknowswhat, add to a relentless string of odd jobs he's done since high school. For the past year or so, he's been doing remote control garage door systems, and that's really taking off. His oldest friend, Kevin Packard makes the sales, and Dobby does the installation, with the assistance of a couple of negro teenagers. He makes a commission, and it's steady work.

He takes a seat on the front porch swing to roll a cigarette. He'll be thirty three this year, a milestone year, year Christ died and all that. Meanwhile, he doesn't even have a garage in which to install a remote control garage door system for himself, parks his truck in the driveway or on the street.

A distant murmur seeps from the wrinkles and cracks of the support beams and gradually creeps closer and clearer, a rough whisper like the wind in a cave. It isn't the first time the house has spoken to him, but he still can't make out what it's trying to say. He tries to put the discomfort out of his mind by turning his attention to the square, manicured lawn. Grass looks a little dry. From behind the shrubs he retrieves a plastic yellow sprinkler attachment, screws it to the end of the nearby hose, and drags it into the center of the yard. He grabs another beer from the refrigerator in the garage on his way to the side yard where he turns on the water. Patrick and a couple of his damn little shithead friends come running from the woods down the road. He makes a note to himself that he'll order a pizza or something later because Patrick is staying over tonight. By turns, the boys leap through the cascades of water. The sharp squeals pierce into Dobby's skull, hammered further by the click, purr and rattle of the sprinkler.

A scene from his own youth jabs him, a fight by the creek that he used to pass every day on the way to school. Must have been about ten, same age as Patrick is now—the age when jumping over a creek is one of the most thrilling and satisfying things you can do. Robbie Healy, who then was a fat kid with a big mouth, had challenged him, for reasons that time has now erased. Just words turning to actions probably. They pushed each other around a bit, and Dobby ended up with wet shoes and pants when he tripped backwards over a rock and fell in the water, Kevin and that Edwin Bronson just standing there looking at him. He shakes off the memory, even as he can still feel the bitterness of it tensing up his temples.

But then, while his mind is wandering in that direction, he's hit quickly by more memories, flashing one after another: an embarrassing loss when he was on the wrestling team in high school, a flubbed piano recital where he was so nervous that he knocked his sheet music onto the floor when he tried to turn the page, a wasted teenage party in some cowfield when he drank a bottle of tequila and puked in Gene Herring's new red Thunderbird (Sally holding her brother Gene back and begging him to have mercy).

A tight panic and a deep sickness steal over him. His cigarette has burned down to an awkward nub. Nor can he any longer bear the deadly hot sunlight, and he rushes into the house, the interior of which seems now blurry and unfamiliar. In his delirium, he knocks over the garbage bin, overfull with pizza boxes, causing him to slip, stumble and similarly disrupt the stacks of unopened mail and newspapers piled up on the kitchen counter. The tube, which someone, some version of himself, left on earlier, barrages him with more unbearable noise and light, but he can't turn it off. He runs to the bathroom, pukes, rinses his face in the sink. Still dizzy, he finds his way into the arms of a bright orange Laz-e-Boy chair and passes out.

PART I: HOPE ROAD

Chapter 1

A parade of streetlights under a stale red Mississippi sky illuminates his path. Lamp posts, like the legs of incandescent insects straddled across the highway, march Patrick Alexander away from the bigger-than-it-seems little town of Lyonness, away from Ashley, away from the caterwauling of the neighborhood dogs and chickens. When a man is going crazy, an empty road can give him hope. It's four in the morning. He hasn't thought about where he might be going, but in his army surplus backpack he's carrying two white t-shirts, a gray sweatshirt, an extra pair of jeans, three pairs of socks and three pairs of boxer briefs, just in case he decides not to return home.

Last night after dinner, while they were watching some crap on TV, Ashley out of the blue said that she would probably like being a tree, and this of course was damn nonsense but Patrick took the bait anyway. Trees are stagnant he said. They stand around and then they just die, wither and rot. No Ashley said. Trees stay in one spot yes but that's exactly what allows them to grow more gigantic, not outward like towns, but upwards like cities, feeding the earth with their fingers and drinking from the earth with their toes. They'd finished a bottle of wine, and she was getting loopy.

It wasn't the tree thing so much as what it inevitably led to— Patrick badgering her about her shallow outdated sixties idealism, in hindsight realizing he was being far too sharp with her; Ashley harping on his underachiever job slinging pies at the local pizza shop and how he spends too much of his paycheck on his motorcycle and on pot. Then the familiar cycle began—the defensiveness, more unnecessary meanness, a tightly wound ball of pride, resentment and guilt that for some reason he can't let go. He recognizes all that of course. He'd have to be blind not to. He has flipped through the piles of self-help books that Ashley bought almost compulsively. But he feels instinctively that it will take something stronger than psychobabble to change his life.

Maybe he just can't deal with normal life, normal "reality," whatever that turns out to be. A justification your brain creates for what your senses perceive. He muses that that sounds almost like a koan, the riddle of the Zen Buddhists. Like asking yourself what your face looked like before your parents were born. *Mu.*

Spontaneously, he leaves the road, entering a faint trail through the brush. When he was a boy on a bicycle, a dense thicket of woods always meant the possibility of discovering a doorway to somewhere mysterious and new. On the other side, he'd found at times the hidden neighborhoods where so many invisible people live, in countless rows of concrete houses, or there was suddenly a grocery store, a drug store, an arcade. The worlds of young boys on bicycles are constructed of a series of labyrinths, and the point is not to escape the labyrinth, but to find every possible doorway into the next one. It was also on these trails that all the neighborhood kids used to run loose, stomping out their aggressions in the trees and mud like Celtic warriors, medieval crusaders, grail-questing knights, musketeers, merry men, or whatever game they decided on that day.

Behind a dewy web of weeds and ivy, is it, yes, the old fort. Patrick and a couple of his friends had painstakingly constructed it using the plywood and chicken wire structure from an unused chicken coop in Dorian's uncle's backyard, though they realized later that it might have made more sense to buy new materials. But anyway, it's still standing. That the wood hasn't yet rotted to the point of caving in upon itself is a curious miracle.

He struggles to crawl through the tiny square opening. Hot musty smell of rotting, damp, termite-ridden wood. He wonders if he can sta- . . .

His boot snaps through the floor, slips on the wet leaves and pine straw underneath, and he lands with his ass in a pile of muck. In the corner, he notices a stash of old porn magazines, some weather-faded and forever-glued shut, but others that were fresh and new. The current occupants have cleverly figured out to put them in plastic bags. But here's what he hoped to see; the message scratched into the wall with a pocket knife and then traced with permanent marker had not completely faded.

Bobby
10/6/1987
Dead

Bobby was a co-founder of Patrick's childhood play world, a world Patrick called 'Zen' for reasons he could no longer remember. Bobby was at once a demigod, a brother, and a paragon of all things young Patrick found noble and virtuous. There were other demigods as well—Martians, monkeys and lizards—the kinds of archetypal beings that often stir a youngster's imagination. Patrick and his friends would sit in this chicken coop, and he'd spin yarns of

Bobby and these mythic characters, their adventures solving petty mysteries and fighting minor injustices, for his pals' entertainment. Though they were fictions, at nine Patrick would have sworn up and down that they were at least as real as Jesus. He had 'faith' in them (as he recalls from his year and a half as a philosophy major at the University of Alabama, 'faith' was defined by William James as when you believe in something you know isn't true, and though James' intention was undoubtedly ironic, this definition seems to fit Patrick's own view).

He thinks back to those soggy summer evenings when, even from the fort half a mile away from his house, above the adolescent yer deads and yer its, his mother, who had the loudest dinner call in the neighborhood, could be heard singing his name. Her voice would signify the end of the day.

When he stayed at his dad's house, the rules were different. He stayed out as late as he pleased. Hardly saw him when he wasn't passed out in front of the television, sometimes with a cigarette still smoldering in his spotty fingers.

Then Bobby died. Suddenly, mysteriously. That was where Patrick's brain took him, not to gradually grow distant from his imaginary friend, but to kill him off, and to write it down on the wall of the fort, the headquarters of that fictional world—that made it official. There was no going back after that. In this universe of the childgod, everything he ever imagined lived on infinitely in a perfect embodiment of his personal mythology.

What did it look like, his face, before his parents were born?

With no small amount of labor, he frees himself from the plywood structure. One leg out, then the other, scraping his wet ass through the little door. Then, as suddenly and disjointedly as a TV dream sequence, Patrick feels himself in that parallel world of the demigods. The pigments of his surroundings become soft and translucent, as if sketched with colored pencils. He's never thought much about the moon being present at this early hour of the morning, but he takes note of its fullness, peeking bashfully from behind the curtain of copper clouds.

"Lovely of you to visit. No flowers?" That voice, which has a faint Scottish lilt, with a sharp and tinny pitch like a slightly sped-up cassette tape, comes from a familiar green haze that's now materialized in the moon shadow. It belongs to Zord, a commander of the Royal Martian Army, a character from Patrick's old play world. Patrick had originally conceived of this diminutive figment (he's waist high, although naturally, as a specific measurement, "waist high" has evolved as Patrick has aged) as a purveyor of empirical rationality to Earth's underdeveloped civilization, someone who hoped to establish here some consistent form of thought to bring us up to date with the rest of the universe. Zord looks like a three-dimensional rendering of a sketch Patrick might have painted with watercolors when he was ten, so obviously, he's sure this can't really be happening. And yet, there's no denying that he sees the Martian before him, about three feet tall with pointed ears and skin the color and texture of a ripe tomatillo. He has a face on both sides of his head, front and back. In fact, he has no back. He is front on both sides. The little green shit is right there, staring ahead and behind with that look of sage understanding that comes with otherworldliness.

In the next moment, Patrick notices that Monkeyman and Harold are there also. Monkeyman hangs from the limbs of a nearby tree—a thoroughly iconic monkey, with light brown fur, a coconut shaped head and a long tail, roughly four and a half feet tall when standing erect, which he typically doesn't. He leans down and smacks Patrick on the back of the head with a stick. "*Mu.*"

Monkeyman giggles maniacally, like a hyperactive child.

Harold is a man-sized lizard (again, relative), his blood-red skin oozing with a translucent almost semen-like substance. At present, he doesn't speak, but merely looks on, his facial expressions implying only mild curiosity. He snorts a terse giggle at Monkeyman's antics and then goes back to smelling the dewy flowers.

Patrick drinks this in, does not respond to the voices that he's not certain he just heard. The three of them appear holographic, like they could flicker and fade away at any moment. Zord says, "Aren't you at least going to say hello?"

He isn't. He's consciously fighting the absurd urge to challenge the unreal phenomena to somehow prove that they are real. Monkeyman emits a series of terrible, nonsensical simian noises, which Patrick finds disturbing not least because the old Monkeyman, the one he made up, spoke like a human. His chattering is not so much monkey-like as a poor but enthusiastic monkey imitation.

Zord comes closer, looking up at Patrick with empathy. "What brings you here, lad? A new mystery for us to solve? Just feeling nostalgic?"

Harold and Monkeyman both start laughing again.

What brought him here, essentially, was again his identification with life on television, the neatly wrapped up episodes, the commercial breaks. Once in a while, he just wants to change the channel. Admittedly, he has done this a couple of times, and upon returning, Ashley always takes him back in. They each pledge their sincere love for each other, fucked up as they both are sometimes, and they promise that they will try to repair their relationship.

But here he is again.

In Patrick's silence, Zord turns his shoulder away so that neither of his faces looks at Patrick directly. "Of course, you don't have to answer. We all know what it is. I'm only a spectator in this situation, but it's perfectly clear to me that it's because, at your essence, you're a selfish prig. You're an adult, for the love of Pete, with a wife and rent—adult problems. And yet, here you are playing at running away like a petulant child."

Patrick just looks around in discomfort. After a moment, Zord glares at him and then delivers a lugubrious frown.

"Oh, are your feelings hurt? Well, your feelings are nothing more and nothing less than a collection of chemicals swimming around in your brain, so get over it. Perhaps you are familiar with the expression 'feelings aren't facts.' I certainly hope I haven't hurt your facts, because that would be another matter . . . "

"Fuck off."

Patrick's words echo against piles of dead wood as the ghosts disappear into the autumn leaves. A justification your mind creates for what your senses perceive. *Mu.*

Here is a tall magnolia tree, and it begs to be climbed. Patrick grabs the lowest limb and swings himself skyward, feeling himself gaining new strength with each level of height until he can see over the old chicken coop fort and down the trail. He tastes a teardrop off his lip. All the smiling faces of his past are lined up in a plastic procession to take a cannibalistic bite of his soul, and Ashley is first in line. He begs the wind and whatever gods may listen for some hint of just what the hell is going on.

There is suddenly a swift wind, then loud crack, and then a pulsing pain in his head. He lies on the ground weeping for all the sky to see. The sun is now on the horizon, peeking through a layer of fluffy red clouds, but in a matter of minutes, a dark wave comes tumbling into the skyscape. Guttural grunts of thunder grow into explosive crashes. Patrick lies still, his thoughts still racing too quickly to catch, his eyes still focused on the parade of cannibals. It rains.

Chapter 2

This is the parallel universe created by a childgod, where everything exists and nothing dies, where the absurd becomes rational and the rational becomes moot, where a shred of hope becomes a shred of evidence, where spirits dwell and play, where good and evil know no boundaries, where the muses, the angels, and the furies mingle in harmony, where matter is constructed from the most tenuous knowledge. In the great halls of a collective conscience, decorated by the great works of history and literature and philosophy, dilapidated from years of misuse and misunderstanding, silent windows open spontaneously to display the world outside as quickly as an eye can open and shut again. The demigods of this all but abandoned realm—alien, simian and reptilian—huddle around the window and note the entrance of an enigmatic figure in gray trench coat, out on his morning stroll, a habitual creative exercise.

This figure is Stone—a painter, sometimes sculptor, sometimes whatever he has to do to get by. He met Ashley and Patrick when all three were in college. Afterwards, he moved to Lyonness for "no particular reason" (originally) and "the sake of art" (a more recent claim).

Stone counts his breaths, and he tries to think of a pun on "poetic license," but he can't. The rain has been sporadically brutal, but he perseveres. In his pocket, he carries a list of things he has noticed in the past few weeks: a tennis shoe posed atop a large rock, maybe a gravestone for someone's pet; an algae-covered birdbath with a marble fisherman on the ledge, a chunk missing from the fisherman's right leg; the charred cement-block foundation that remains after a house burned down. These are some of the landmarks of his walk. Daily, he notes any changes that occur. None occur.

When his path takes him through a lightly wooded trail, he sees his friend Patrick passed out on the ground.

Through a second window, the view of the demigods passes by the fuzzy orange sofa for which Ashley Alexander paid twelve dollars at a garage sale; by the stereo, television, and DVD player arranged neatly against the wall; through the bead curtain and into the kitchen where last night's dishes are still piled in the sink; down the narrow hallway and into the bedroom; past a Lava Lamp on the dresser, and the demigods hover over the bed like the end of a dream.

The alarm clock/radio/telephone beeps nasally, 6:45 a.m. A tanned and svelte arm stretches out from underneath the covers, pawing for the switch to turn off the alarm. Ashley lies still for a few minutes, tented by the sheets, and then begins to roll around in vain attempts to surface into the awake world. Shit, she mumbles as she rolls over into Patrick's empty space.

She sits up suddenly, blonde curls matted against her face. She looks quickly around for signs of him: boots, jacket, backpack.

All missing. Well, fuck him. It sounds like there's a terrible storm outside, one of those leonine rains of early March. She jumps out of bed and pulls back the paisley curtains she made from fabric she found in her parents' basement. Outside gale forces pull twigs and dead leaves past the window, bending the tops of the pines in a mystic dance.

Fuck him. She hopes he dies. Don't think about it, make breakfast. She's starving.

She turns on a stove burner, sprays a skillet down with non-fat cooking spray, cracks an egg into the pan. She puts two pieces of rye bread in the toaster oven. While her bread browns and her egg sizzles, she mixes up brown breakfast shake powder with skim milk. She swallows a bright orange multi-vitamin pill, washes it down with the shake then takes the bread out of the toaster oven, spreads low-fat peanut butter across one slice, plops the fried egg on top of that and makes a sandwich. Wrapping this in a paper towel, she carries her breakfast into the living room.

She turns on the stereo and starts the tape of Josh's band, the Lost Expletives. Terrible name. Josh told her once that he chose the band name because, in his view, they represented something profane, vulgar yet not recognized as such, not unlike the forgotten vernacular of an ancient working class. Or something like that. Great band though. Or maybe she's just sentimental. The Lost Expletives played at their wedding.

She lights a joint and thinks about a time when Patrick wasn't a psycho, or at least not so obviously, or maybe she was just as crazy as he was. They used to take acid or ecstacy and go to the library in the middle of the night, keys stolen from Patrick's librarian mother, wandering from aisle to aisle in awe of the dense and enormous quantity of information. Patrick would open a book at random and the words would blend together into a great soup of text from which they would slurp phrases as they came to life.

But fuck him, now. She hopes he dies. She falls almost to sleep. Her eyes are heavy, watery, and she lies back on the ochre sofa, cooled and calmed by the mild whisper of the ceiling fan, a marigold in the wind. No sooner, though, is she reclined in a slumberous position than the doorbell rings. She swallows what's left of her breakfast shake, and, leaping to peek through the peephole, sees Stone struggling to hold up a limp body. She opens the door.

"I have a package here for Ashley Alexander."

"God, you're soaked. Come in and dry off."

Stone drags Patrick, dripping, into the den.

"Put him on the couch, I guess," she says. "You can get some clean clothes for yourself out of Patrick's dresser. It's the tall one in the corner."

Ashley runs to get towels out of the closet. She throws one to Stone in the bedroom and then goes to Patrick, removing his jacket, boots, shirt, and pants, drying him thoroughly. His skin reeks of whiskey. She covers him with a blanket and puts a pillow under his head. Then she decides to make coffee. While she is grinding the beans, Stone comes out of the bedroom in shorts and shirt of Patrick. In the borrowed clothes, he looks foreign, not like himself or like Patrick, just a handsome and comfortably familiar stranger.

"What the hell happened to him? Was he with you?"

"No. I found him passed out in the woods. He might just be drunk. Obviously, he's drunk. But I don't think he was mugged or anything. He had his wallet and his backpack still. I don't know what he was doing out there, especially in this weather."

"What were you doing out there?"

"I was there for the sake of art . . . You want to see my poetic license?"

"Very funny. Want some coffee?"

"Sure, thanks. Black is fine."

She pours and watches Stone in the den, brushing Patrick's hair out of his face, tender in his affection for his friend. "Has he said anything?"

"No, but he has a nasty bump on his head. You might want to get it checked out."

As they both sip their coffee, gazing upon Patrick with a sort of helpless empathy, he stirs, mumbles something about climbing a tree. Had she said she wanted to be a tree? Time locks in intervals smaller than atoms. The cosmic tick. You can't count that fast, can't see that quickly. Trees outside sway in the mystic wind, ancient as druids. How many atoms a second? Who knows, but better to measure by something tangible like the seasons or the orbits.

Patrick grimaces, seems to be trying to get up. Ashley goes to him, places her long, red-tipped fingers on his chest.

"You need to lie back down, Patrick. Do you feel like telling me what happened?"

His voice is stilted and gruff from being in the rain and lacking sleep. Ashley notices a little dried blood on the pillow. It's worse than she thought.

"Jesus, what the fuck have you done to yourself?"

"I had this idea . . . fuck, my head hurts . . . Shit."

"Okay, don't move. I'm calling in to work, and then I'll take you to the emergency room."

Stone volunteers to come along to the hospital, and Ashley is glad. She takes a final swig of her coffee, and the stereophonic clamor of the Lost Expletives comes into the foreground for just a moment. She turns down the stereo and goes in the kitchen to make the phone call, inhaling the smell of the garbage piling up and the dishes that need to be washed and the floor that needs to be mopped and the oven that needs to be cleaned and the mice. Answering machine . . .

"Thank you for calling Sunny-Side Up Tanning Salon. We can't answer the phone at the moment, but please leave a message or call back during regular business hours."

"Oh, hi. This is Ashley. I might be late today. I have to take Patrick to the emergency room; he hit his head on something."

The phone call ends with a click.

. . . and the window of the demigods closes like an eye in the rain.

Chapter 3

Wait for the final drops to drip yellow into the water. When they first married he asked Ashley to watch. Wanted to be comfortable doing anything in front of her because they were living as one organism. Would have liked to drink hers, have her drink his, like blood brotherhood. He'd suggested it as part of their wedding ceremony, but the idea was flatly vetoed. She wouldn't do it, and he stopped pushing for it, but he still keeps the door open.

Sometimes it's completely clear and sometimes more yellow—he wonders which is better. This time very yellow, lots of sediment, smells bitter. His head hurts still, but he can go to work. It's been a few days since the fall.

Harold the lizard sits on the top of the toilet tank, a muted red blur. Patrick ignores this, flushes. He washes down some ibuprofen with water from the tap, and then he shaves in long, ritualistic strokes. For a second, in the steam-diffused medicine cabinet mirror, he sees Monkeyman's coconut-shaped head, and then his own face returns.

Why is that old universe re-awakening, he wonders.

Harold follows him out of the bathroom into the hallway,

leaving behind a faint trail of slime that evaporates almost instantly. This is just some kind of brain pollution, brain noise, he thinks. In a somber mood, he dons his old fedora. Black with a white ribbon band, this fedora is of the type commonly found in costume shops and theme parks, and according to its label, manufactured from a material dubiously called 'durafelt.' Patrick purchased his at Busch Gardens in Tampa while on vacation with his mother when he was a teenager. He's worn it ever since.

He leaves the house.

This is the land created by a childgod, where everything exists and nothing dies.

The chickens from the yard next door follow him part of the way down the block. He turns down past the Episcopal Church of the Incarnation, where his mother is probably right now cleaning up the kitchen from the Parish brunch. He still gets slightly spooked whenever he is pressured by her to go there for a Christmas Eve service, wedding or funeral. Interesting building though, with its stony exterior, tall stained glass windows, the oddly designed underground passageway from the choir room to the chapel, and the even more oddly placed storage rooms. Series of labyrinths, everything is.

He jumps the fence into the church playground and notices that the demigods are still following him, lazing in the swing set, inhabiting all the possible worlds. He jumps the other side of the fence, skips down a grassy hill and enters woods, steps over a narrow creek to a short trail—another door, another maze.

He crushes leaves under his feet, trying to be lighter, looking for an experience or a series of events that would make him more than what he is, a body in motion through space, wondering if he will collide with something.

The trail comes out at a grassy park on the edge of town. A flock of pigeons scrambles into the air at the sound of his footsteps. Demigods disperse into the shadows. Children, slide, race, and jump over the ditch that runs through the middle of the park, as he remembers doing. Old couples eat fried chicken at the picnic tables, and a group of shirtless teenagers at the other end throws a Frisbee™ back and forth. Parading cycles of life. Cannibals. Ugh. 2:15 . . . Still early. He sits down in the grass to smoke a cigarette.

". . . Mother was an avid reader before she died . . ."

This pronouncement is emitted via a loud and nasal female voice, from a group of four young women picnicking on a large rock under a fig tree. They are drinking wine from plastic cups, and one of them is holding a knife. Another is eating a pickle spear.

". . . All my brothers and sisters also, avid readers . . ."

The one with a knife begins to cut a loaf of French bread and pass the slices around.

"What did they read?"

"Oh, mysteries and romances mostly. I mean they read all the classics, but after that they read whatever they could get their hands on."

"Nobody's read all the classics . . ."

He is listening to them, not listening to them, listening more to the sun and the grass. Ant crawling over his shoe. Blow smoke on the ant. Drives him crazy. Probably gets him high.

". . . There are too many classics to read all of them . . ."

Too many indeed, he thinks. Overflow of information. It's a definition of an age, information highway and all that. He's always been envious of people who know more than him, of a conspiracy of intellectuocracy, Gnostic government, knowledge worship, literary critics like superheroes. Always wanted to be a prodigy, but always ends up a prodigal son . . .

Patrick picks himself up and moves on through the town . . . the town, the town, the highway, 'nother town down the way, high down the way. Any resemblance between this town and similar towns is merely the way folks are constructed here in Southern America where it is jungle hot, and them contrarebels are preparing for the intellectual revolution, meeting in the basement of Vanzetti's pizzeria to make secret plans, read poetry, listen to politically energized punkrock CDs. Must work, make big money, pay for motorcycle and houserent or bigtitty wife get angry and suspicious.

Why'd he ever get married anyway, he thinks? He thought he was for free love and individualism, and somehow he got caught up in this . . . institution. Never recommends it to any of his friends. Still he lusts and masturbates with sometimes alarming frequency, and, in a way, he prefers illicit affairs and self-pleasure to sex with the wife. He wonders why she hasn't taken another lover.

He enters the back door of Vanzetti's and ties on the familiar tomato stained white apron. Then he begins sorting frozen bags of shredded cheese into plastic buckets. As he does this, Monkeyman sits in lotus position across from him, his little monkey face in placid repose.

"Focus on your breath. Breathe in the essence of your Being."

Patrick is a little annoyed at this. Nevertheless, he has always found menial tasks in the kitchen to be both meditative and calming, so he ignores the monkey specter. Before long, his mind is empty, and Monkeyman has vanished.

After the cheese buckets are filled, he mixes a bucket of pizza sauce, stirring in a bag of pre-mixed spices with a large rubber spatula. He stands up at a counter to cut some green peppers. As he slices them, he focuses his eyes on a poster riddled with unintentionally ironic quotation marks.

5 Essentials of Success:
1. Provide "Fast Service"
2. Serve "Top Quality Product"
3. Maintain the "Highest Standards of Cleanliness"
4. Display "Genuine Courtesy"
5. Meet or exceed guest expectations by delivering "Dependable Consistency"

Through the thin wall that separates him from the front part of the restaurant, Patrick hears someone come in. Then he hears the shop's owner, Nick Vanzetti—who is at the counter adding up receipts, making calculations—greeting with his usual strained tolerance Alvin, a regular afternoon visitor but not a customer.

Alvin receives disability because of some sort of mental illness. He lived in a number of half-way houses in Tupelo until his parents died, leaving him a large house on the edge of Lyonness. A social worker checks in with him from time to time, and it has been several years since his last psychotic episode. Short, thin, balding, unshaven, always smoking a cigarette, effeminate, middle aged, Alvin comes in at least once every day just to say hi, and maybe visit for a while to get out of the heat or use the restroom. Speaking with the gentility of a Southern belle, Alvin launches into one of his trademark rambling stories.

"The oddest thing just happened to me. I was walking down the street, and this young man says 'Hey come over here.' And I thought it was my friend Fred, but Fred has this young lover named Wayne. Anyway, I said to him 'Come down to the laundromat with me and smoke a cigarette' and he followed me down there. Well, I was introducing him to Maggie, the young girl who works at the laundromat, and I said 'Maggie, this is Fred.' And he said 'Fred? I'm Wayne, not Fred.' I was so embarrassed."

At the pause, Nick responds, as Patrick expected he would, with a noncommittal grunt. Then the phone rings and Nick answers, taking an order. After he hangs up, he asks Alvin to hold on a second.

"Patrick! I need a large olive and mushroom."

"Well, anyway, to continue my tale of woe, this young man told me that he was fixin' to go down to Foley Park." As Patrick turns the corner, he sees Alvin looking knowingly at Nick and Nick looking unknowingly back at Alvin. "Oh, there you are. How are you today?"

"Fine, and you?"

"Oh, I'm well. I was just telling your friend that a young man told me he was going down to Foley Park, he said, to try to pick up about thirty bucks. Well, I'd heard that young men go down to that park and sell their bodies, but I can't believe this boy had the nerve to tell me that, as if he wanted me to come along. I think he thought I had money or something. Can I use your facilities?"

"Sure thing. You know where it is."

When Alvin comes out of the bathroom, he is giggling to himself.

"Do y'all think I could make any money down at that park?" Alvin models his body for them. "What do y'all think? Am I marketable?"

Nick looks up. "There are some things that I don't even speculate about."

Chapter 4

Ashley feels the space between Patrick and herself stretching like the spandex-fabric of time. The universe drifts asunder and she's noticed Patrick's orbit gradually expanding to a wider and longer oval, cooling and hardening as the gravity of home loosens its grip. Ashley lights the house, waters the plants, warms a frozen dinner in the oven. She mixes herself a chocolate breakfast shake. Billions of tiny explosions every second.

She hears the screen door slam shut, and he enters, insouciant as a balloon in the Macy's day parade on TV.

"Your dinner's in the oven."

"Yeah? Great, what are we having?" He hugs her affectionately from behind.

"I'm having a diet milkshake thing like I have every night. You are having some Swedish meatballs and fettuccini, complements of Budget Gourmet. Where have you been smoking pot?"

"Does it smell?" He is pungent. She nods. "I got off work early and ran into Josh. His band's playing tonight at The Club, and he said he'd put us on the guest list."

The Club, an anomaly in the quiet, rural town of Lyonness, is located in the back of a liquor store, and it is, above all, just a dive bar, but there is a small stage where bands sometimes perform. Typically, these are either young teenage speed metal bands or middle-aged blues bands, often on the same night. Josh and the other members of the Lost Expletives are the sole example of twenty-something "alternative" bands that play this venue. The band actually relocated to Birmingham (about two hours away) some time ago, but they still play their hometown bar a few times a year.

She looks at him for the first time since he came home. He seems to have gotten smaller. In art, that's called perspective.

"Okay, that sounds fun."

She scoops the fettuccini from the cardboard box onto a plate. He eats quickly, allowing no time for the noodles to cool. When he finishes, he puts his plate in the sink, discards the cardboard box into the garbage can and starts looking in the refrigerator.

Dissatisfied, Ashley hovers into the next room and turns on the television. Nothing is on except local news. She leaves it on, lights a ginseng cigarette, sifts through the junk mail.

...AND NOW, WRDN NEWS CORRESPONDENT, CHARITY RODGERS, IN AN EXCLUSIVE INTERVIEW WITH SENATOR EDWIN BRONSON...

Oh Charity, Ashley silently laments. What have you done to your hair? It didn't used to be so puffy and tall. She sips her shake and takes a drag off the cigarette. The summer frock she wore to work comes off. Takes off her bra and tosses it onto the couch. Her shoes are already off. She throws the mail in the garbage, sits down on the couch, and drinks the last grainy drops of her shake. Is this what she has become, she wonders. A lump on the sofa, waiting? For Patrick? To do something? God.

. . . SENATOR, IN THE AFTERMATH OF THE HURRICANE THAT DEVASTATED THIS AREA A FEW MONTHS AGO, YOU'VE BEEN ACCUSED OF BEING OVERLY GENEROUS WITH THE TAXPAYERS' MONEY, HANDING OUT NO BID CONTRACTS TO CRONIES. HOW DO YOU ANSWER THESE ALLEGATIONS? . . .

In the bathroom, she digs in the laundry basket for a tee shirt and some jeans, and her naked reflection catches her eye. She is bronze as an academy award, as a penny, as a third-place medal. Has he lost interest in her? Maybe he's having an affair, she thinks. If he were, he would probably be really obvious about it. He can't hide things. He would talk about her, flirt with her in front of me.

. . . DOES IT NOT REFLECT BADLY ON YOUR CONSTITUENTS IF YOU . . .

She hears Patrick in the other room, shuffling around, breathing. She dresses.

. . . SENATOR, WHO IS SERVED BY THIS POLICY? . . .

In Ashley's car, a white '94 Sunbird that her parents gave her when she graduated high school—the crimson and gold tassel still hangs from the rear view mirror—they travel silently together to the club, The Club. The streets that surround the town square are saturated with election signs, mostly for the incumbent Senator Bronson. Cracked glass and black pebbles cover the parking lot. The night is unusually arid. As they enter, a giant mural looms above, a reclining woman with pointy and angular curves and a flaming red pelvis, painted by Stone during his pointy, flaming woman period.

Lips banter indistinguishably over musky glasses, and the rhythm of the drums shakes the room slightly, tingles their spines. Some members of the audience form a fleshy pulp around the front of the stage, trying to dance, but they are too closed in. They stagger as a group, holding each other up with their sweaty bodies. Josh is singing a punk rock non-melody

Life sucks. People suck.
Life sucks. People suck.
Fuck it all. Fuck it all.
I need a good fuck.

The music pounds through an instrumental section. Patrick goes to get them beers. Ashley watches the band, amused by their rock antics. All four figures on the stage are thrashing around frantically. Fish, the lead guitar player, is bouncing up and down. Louie beats the shit out of his drums with meticulous precision. James, the bass player, slaps the strings of his instrument and wags his tongue in careless ecstasy. Each time Josh takes up the microphone, he sneers like a wild coyote.

Reality sucks. Fantasy sucks.
Reality sucks. Fantasy sucks.
Fuck it all. Fuck it all.
I need a faster car.

Louie breaks a stick and grabs another out of his bag without missing a beat. Without missing a beat. Without missing a beat.

Life sucks. Death sucks.
Life sucks. Death sucks.

Fuck it all. Fuck it all.
I'm gonna be a shepherd.

Patrick returns with beers, and they each grab chairs. She shouts to him, "Louie's a really good drummer, isn't he?"

Her comment is answered with the patronizing look Patrick always gives her when she says something he considers inane, obvious or moot.

A busty teen named Cherry Hindersen greets them, yelling above the music. Cherry is probably seventeen, zaftig, with a square Germanic face. Whenever they see her, which is all too often for Ashley's comfort, she bombards them with her scandalous tales of teenage promiscuity and decadence.

This week her hair is sort of green and orange. Ashley recalls that last week it was a vampyric red. Her white denim jacket is covered with buttons; one says, "Anarchy Rules." So lame, artificial, thinks Ashley. They are only friends because this is a small town and everybody knows most everybody else, especially if you're under thirty and you have any clue about what's going on in the rest of the world. The few young people stick close together, and some, like Patrick and Ashley, are reluctant to give up their youth well into their twenties and thirties. When the song ends and she can speak without yelling, Cherry says, "So, you know I'm living in a house with three guys now? Two of them are drug dealers. I mean they carry guns around and shit."

Ashley catches herself rolling her eyes. She searches deeply to find some empathy for Cherry so she can join the conversation. "Jesus, that must be scary. I don't like guns."

"Yeah, well it is sometimes, and you know, I don't like the guns in the house, but you know, if they shoot each other, they'll deserve it, and if they shoot me, I won't be around to complain about it, so I guess it really doesn't make any difference."

"But what if you, like, get shot and don't die?"

Cherry laughs. "That's just the sort of thing that would happen to me."

Ashley isn't impressed with Cherry's faux-nihilism, and it really piques her when Patrick interjects his opinion of the matter.

"At least you're getting laid, huh?"

"Yeah."

Ashley gets up and walks to the restroom. She splashes some cold water on her face. The universe is a dark place. A faint light reflects her face in the mirror, a few inches away, but still a fraction of a second in the past. She cannot even see herself as she really is, much less Patrick. She wonders how long it takes the light to arrive from the sun.

When she emerges, Josh is singing a different song, one of the older pretty ones that she always liked. Fish's guitar feeds back transcendently. The bass and drums crash in. Patrick and Cherry are talking and laughing. They seem so much smaller than she.

Chapter 5

Patrick has trouble sleeping, and so goes naked into the kitchen and turns on the light, squinting at the brightness for a few seconds while his eyes adjust. The hazy blue microwave LCD shows 5:10. In the refrigerator, he finds some bread, some milk, a platter of turkey, some candy left over from Easter, about seven weeks old. When his knife pierces the thigh of the turkey, the plastic handle breaks off, but he still manages to scrape off some meat. Sits down to make a sandwich, thinking of the Blondie comic strip, how Dagwood's sandwiches are always so big that you can't even make yourself imagine him trying to fit his mouth over it to take a bite.

Hey where's the paper? He's not sure when it gets delivered. Wonders should he put on a towel? Nobody's around or awake, fuck it, just check.

Patrick takes a step outside into the cool gray of early dawn, smell of grass wet with dew, and within seconds the newspaper lands at his naked feet, accompanied by catcalls and whistles from the black sedan from which it was ejected. He kneels down to pick it up, and a heron flying overhead startles him with its call. He sees it soar upward toward a hole in the cloud cover. Another storm is coming. On the way back inside, he weeds out the advertising sections and throws them away. He skims the news.

Photo on the front page shows a thin man, big-eyes, middle-aged, shot in New York yesterday. Patrick guesses he was from this area, originally. Carter. Never heard of him. Ethics charges against Senator Bronson. Mississippi politics slippery as a baby water moccasin. No big surprises in that section really. There's flooding in the delta; a car crashed through the front window at Bargain Town; there's a street fair this weekend that will more than likely get rained out.

Turns to the comics. Blondie. He's been told that he looks something like Dagwood—same hair. Eerie, but unlike Patrick and Ashley, Dagwood and Blondie have a perfect marriage, living in a two-story house in a quaint suburb with two kids that look exactly like them (even the dog looks like them), steady jobs, neighbors who borrow their tools. Too big to swallow—like a cartoon sandwich. Patrick, on the other hand, has no lettuce or tomato, not even mustard or mayonnaise, not an olive or a pickle in sight, dry wheat bread with slices of turkey, seven-week-old chocolate for dessert.

He nibbles on the dry sandwich, and the sun begins to come up, beaming through the screened window. As the sunbeam creeps closer, it slowly transforms into the giant red lizard, Harold. Patrick has started to grow accustomed to this. He doesn't take a second look.

He needs a cup for his milk; they are all dirty. He digs through the pile of dishes in the sink, looking for a glass to rinse out. The janiform Martian, Zord, appears and points one out to him, a yellow one, hidden underneath the dishtowel. "Thanks."

"Can't sleep, eh?"

"I'm getting very restless. My motorcycle is paid off now. Everything seems to be in order. Ashley and I aren't getting along. I'm thinking about hitting the road."

Zord looks at him with suspicion. Patrick looks back at him with disbelief. Zord is fat and has a hairy belly. How'd he get fat? Zord spits a little when he talks, and Patrick has to be on guard against the alien saliva.

"Uh, hmm. So what exactly do you think is 'in order?'" As he does when he is irritated, Zord begins swinging his penis around like a lasso.

"Look, it's different this time. I have a lot of things to figure out."

The main thing he has to figure out is not something he can't get rid of; it's something he's lost. Something foggy and spiritual. Something that transcends everything in his small and ordinary universe, which is necessarily something not of that universe, something to make his life sacred.

"You're starting to sound dangerous. You have no idea what you're doing. I don't think you should go anywhere right now."

"I've already made up my mind."

"Damn your mind. Define your terms. You don't even know what a mind is. It's nonsense. You sound as bad as that blasted monkey. But tell me this. Is your conscience clear?"

"Conscience? Where do you get off talking about a conscience? Isn't that as much within the taboo realm of the metaphysical as the 'mind?'"

"You think I can't explain consciousness! I fart on your consciousness, you Hegelian twerp. Answer me, damn it."

Patrick wonders if he should write a note. Never has before, but that's all the more reason to write one now.

He finds a pad and pencil, and scribbles some meaningless shapes. He can't find words, language eluding him this morning. He tears off the page and throws it away, leaving the yellow plastic cup on top of the blank pad.

He goes to get his clothes. Ashley sleeps heavily. He tries not to look at her, silently puts on some boxer shorts and pants, pulls on his boots and a white tee shirt. Finding his backpack, he stuffs in some extra shirts, shorts, socks, toothbrush, and a comb. She hasn't moved.

Zord begins to be even more irritated.

"Why don't you answer me?"

For a moment, Patrick is afraid the imaginary alien will wake her; then he remembers. He leaves the room. In the garage, he eyes the motorcycle, the mighty steed he has selected for his quest, the Yamaha VMAX 1200, burgundy, a power king. He puts on his leather jacket, zipping it up ceremoniously. The giant red lizard is there, as is Monkeyman, and of course, Zord. The monkey has his thick simian hair groomed for the occasion, having just spent the last several hours picking the bugs out of his beard. His mood is somber.

The cast lines up, clad in all their most celebratory apparel in a salute to send Patrick off on his journey. Monkeyman, wearing a blue corset and hat with matching stockings all bejeweled with various precious stones, blows a trumpet.

Harold, dressed in like manner, begins reading from a scroll.

"Let it be hereby thtated, that yay whipperthnapper in full blethed uniform ith heretofore rethigned to ethtablishing under thome thircumthtanceth a rationale for idiothyncrathieth under which he hath therewhat endured for nigh thix and twenty revolutionth of the celethtial lightgiver and thereby retholved to interfathe with thuch dangerth ath he might intercounter by the way and that under the thircumthtanceth of which he doeth not return to thith thame thpot after the duration of one thuch revolution as therebefore mentioned with the addition of one thmaller rotation of the orb which he interhabitateth then he hereby claimth the right to thurrender unto this court whatever punishment it may render meet for him et thetera."

Monkeyman interperets. "In other words, you have a year to figure out what is wrong with you. After that, you will come back, and if you've made no decisions, we'll make a decision for you."

Patrick puts on his helmet. Zord, looking directly at him and directly away from him. "You are making a mistake, and a common one at that! What you're looking for is not something you can claim like a trophy."

Patrick is not discouraged. He pushes the bike down the road, not wanting Ashley to hear the motor and discover him gone too soon. After a block, he starts the engine, taking whatever road likes him best.

Chapter 6

Demigods in transit.

Through telephone wires and sewage pipes, along the Burlington Northern Santa Fe Railroad, the Norfolk Southern Railroad, and the CSX Transportation railway, along the Tenn-Tom waterway, the Tennessee River, and the Black Warrior River, along Interstate 20/59, Interstate 65, U.S. 78, U.S. 82, U.S. 31 and U.S. 280.

This is Birmingham. Steel mills form a jagged-toothed grimace across the skyline in the north. To the belly of the city, overseen from the south by the great cast iron statue of Vulcan, steel smith of the Roman gods, where rows of housing projects, sparsely populated office buildings and dead warehouses occupy what used to be the heart of downtown, where fire hoses once drenched black kids, where churches were exploded, where Martin Luther King was jailed. On the south side, just below the two sets of railroad lines that gave birth to the city, there is the University of Alabama-Birmingham and its affiliated hospital, the rising star of the area's economic future. Nearby, there are bars and restaurants, parks and playgrounds, and middle-class homes, as well as cheaper housing where many college students live.

In that once-rich enclave known as the South Highlands is a pregnant ovoid block nested like an aerie at the top of a steep hill, and in the center of the circle, a gaudy apartment complex with orange and green doors like a 1970s roadside motel looms over the hill. Around the corner are the remains of a house taken apart from the inside out by its previous occupants, the Sigma Nu fraternity from the University of Alabama-Birmingham. Most of the rest of the street is occupied by two and three-story houses, except for a second apartment building, red brick, where a female form silhouettes a second story window streetside.

Rebecca Halley is halfway dressed, thinking about the myth of motherhood. She grew up believing that all women are naturally mothers. Rebecca, however, is mother only to *Cacophony*, a bi-monthly literary arts magazine on its last legs. Nothing is happening. Less than two years ago, out of restlessness, she quit a relatively cushy editorial job at the lone local major magazine publisher, Oxmoor House, and now the same nothing is happening again. Nothing for her, nothing for the wheezing 'zine, nothing for this all-but-illiterate city, nothing for her again. She stares at the vanity mirror in her bedroom, and she decides that a drastic change is in order.

Twisting her fingers around in her long, straight, black hair, she thinks that may be a start—symbolic of a greater spiritual revolution, ceremonial, like Buddhist monks. She reaches for her scissors and cuts before she thinks better of the idea. After just a few snips, she already feels different. The result is not exactly what she had in mind, but she figures she can get Victoria, her co-publisher, to clean it up before the party. Meantime, she has to brush her teeth, finish getting dressed, put on her game face for Birmingham's dilettanti.

The party, which is going to be at the *Cacophony* office, a large old house near downtown, is for the release of what might be the last issue, unless they can manage to solicit some new talent and, more importantly, some funding. Meanwhile, Rebecca and

Victoria are paying for the party out of pocket. Victoria is moving to Florida in a few weeks. So, okay, something is happening. Rebecca is simply not looking forward to taking on the entire project herself, especially to cater to the same old mediocre poets and photographers.

Rebecca arrives early, seeing some interns from U.A.B. cleaning up for the party. She glides into the production room where Victoria is stripping flats and archiving material from the issue just printed. Paste-up is a long-outdated layout method, but it's the only way she and Victoria know how to do it. Even the interns have made snide comments about it.

"What are you doing? You're going to get filthy."

Victoria doesn't look up from her task. "I know, I just can't help myself."

"Do you think you can take a couple of minutes off work and straighten up my hair?"

"Oh God!" Victoria says, finally looking at her. "Who did this to you?"

"Don't be typical. I did it myself. But I need you to straighten out the ends."

Victoria is not a woman to hesitate, especially when accused of being typical. She grabs some scissors out of a drawer and neatly trims Rebecca's hair into something more or less resembling a bob. The black snippets float gently down to the floor joining scraps of paper and pencil shavings.

Rebecca brushes herself off and then jets over to the utility closet to get a broom.

Meanwhile, Victoria puts some bottles of cheap white wine in a cooler of ice, and some interns set out trays of food. Another intern arrives in a pickup truck with two kegs and sets them up on the front porch.

Rebecca puts copies of the new issue out on display. They came off the press yesterday, and she hasn't even looked at them yet.

Victoria said they all looked perfect, but Rebecca finds that nearly impossible to believe. Victoria's standards are always lower than her own. She gets a glass of wine because she wants to be well on her way to drunk before the guests arrive.

She sits in a corner browsing through the pages, sipping at her glass. She has read every one of these pieces at least ten times, but there is something different about them when they're finally in print, everything so neatly arranged and official-looking. She has to admit that the issue ended up looking surprisingly good, notwithstanding a couple of irritating typos she now notices for the first time.

The first guests begin to arrive: Betty Grogan, a cranky old art critic from the *Post Herald*; G. K. with his video camera and copies of his poets' newsletter; and a group of four teenagers in baggy hemp garb. One of the teenagers, a slightly overweight girl named Sundae Robinson, has a poem in the magazine. Rebecca sees Victoria greet Sundae politely, telling her that several people will be reading from their work later on and asking if she would read her poem. Sundae says she'll think about it.

More guests appear at the door, people Rebecca doesn't even know. The front room begins to fill with people eating, drinking, and talking. Victoria puts a mix tape in the stereo, a compilation of free jazz and neo-classical pieces. The office is getting crowded, so she goes outside to get some air and another glass of wine. Kyle Fische, the featured photographer of this issue, comes up to her, wearing a yellow and green jump suit and bright red horn-rimmed glasses. He is bald on top, and two golden wings of blonde hair span out from the sides of his head. "The magazine looks great."

"Thanks. So you got your copy?"

"Yes, ma'am. Have it right here."

He taps the shoulder bag at his side. Kyle's photographs aren't really very interesting, but he's independently wealthy, and he's been supportive of the arts in Birmingham for several years. Gives money to the Birmingham Arts Association and other local groups. She has nothing left to say. The only thing to do is feed their fragile egos. "Great. That series from Sloss Furnace was brilliant. Very industrial."

"Thank you. I do my best."

"Excuse me, I see someone inside I need to talk to."

She slips into the next room and quickly turns the corner so that Kyle won't see that she isn't actually talking to anybody. Then she notices this guy—someone she's never seen before. He seems to be having some sort of argument with Victoria while simultaneously flipping through back issues. He has a demonic gleam, acne scars on his face, wild hair, wearing an army jacket and boots. Kind of scrawny and wiry-looking. She can't figure out where he must have come from. As she approaches, she gleans that they're having some sort of debate about capital punishment.

". . . Would you pull the switch?"

"For God's sake, that's irrelevant. Oh, hi Rebecca. That reminds me, I have to, um, get some more ice."

Victoria excuses herself, making a face privately to Rebecca, signifying her gratitude. Rebecca extends her hand to the stranger.

"Hi, I'm Rebecca Halley. I'm the co-publisher of the magazine. And you are?"

The guy changes gears, his face lights up, and suddenly there's almost a cuteness and a reckless innocence to him, a wicked sense of spontaneity. He shakes the handful of back issues at her. "Glad to meet you. Listen. I, uh, think I want to work with this paper. It looks like you need me."

"Um. It's more of a magazine than a paper, but anyway . . . What sort of thing do you think you'd like to do?"

"I don't know. Help read submissions, separate the wheat from the chaff. And I have some design ideas, although I don't have much experience with that kind of stuff."

"Well, I can get you an application . . ."

"I just want to volunteer."

"Um, we're all volunteers, or interns, except Vic and I and Ron, who does the ad sales. I still would prefer for you to fill out an application. It's mainly so we have a record of your contact information, and we can call you when we need your help with something."

It's also so she can politely blow him off if he turns out to be some kind of nutjob. She disappears into her office to get the form before he can interrupt her again. Where does this asshole get off suddenly blurting out that we need him, she thinks; I probably shouldn't be so accommodating, but we could stand a change of any kind around here so why not give it a shot.

In a minute or two, she returns with the form and a pen. "Is this information really necessary?"

He is pointing to the first blank, the one for his name.

"What's the problem? Are you wanted by the F.B.I.? Come on. We won't tell on you."

He reluctantly fills out the form and hands it back to her. Before she can look at it, he taps her on the arm.

"Listen. A friend of mine is in a band playing this weekend. You ought to come check it out."

He hands her a card and then leaves. The card is a pocket-sized flyer.

Lost Expletives
Saturday Night
Danny Brewer's Farmhouse
$3 cover

On the other side, a map. Looks like this place is way out in the suburbs. Strange place for a band to be playing. She puts the card in her pocket and then looks at the application. She notices that he filled in the first blank, Name, with "An Entity." She tries to look around for him, but he is already gone.

Kyle passes through the room announcing that the reading will begin shortly. "Weird poetry! Wild stuff coming up in two and a half minutes in the main room. Weird poetry!"

Chapter 7

. . . A COMMUNITY IN NORTHEAST MISSISSIPPI WAS DISTURBED TODAY WHEN A STATE PROSECUTOR INDICTED MISSISSIPPI STATE SENATOR EDWIN BRONSON ON CHARGES OF BRIBERY . . .

Dorian, at whose house Patrick has been crashing for a few weeks, carries a tray inside from the patio. "The burgers are ready."

Leaving the television on, Patrick wanders into the kitchen. Dorian puts the tray of vegetarian hamburgers on the counter, while his wife, Karen, tosses together a salad. They all sit down to eat at three sides of the small kitchen table, joining hands to say the blessing. Patrick has to stretch to reach Karen's hand.

It would never occur to Patrick to pray over his food. Before he left Lyonness, eating had become a source of tension with Ashley.

But, he thinks, if anything is sacred still, it is the process of eating, something organic. Something that involves the body. This thought makes him a little more comfortable with the ritual.

Dorian closes his eyes, prays simply, Lord bless this food, etc. He seems sincere about it, and to his own surprise, Patrick finds himself moved. They eat for a minute or so in silence.

. . . AUTHORITIES ARE CURRENTLY INVESTIGATING SENATOR   BRONSON'S   CONNECTION   WITH   A CONSTRUCTION COMPANY IN HIS HOME STATE AND WHETHER WAS TAKING KICKBACKS ON NO-BID STATE CONTRACTS. IN THE MEANTIME, BRONSON HAS NOT BEEN SEEN AT HIS HOME OR OFFICE IN OVER A WEEK . . .

"Oh, you know what I've been meaning to tell you. A few weeks ago, I stumbled across our fort."

"The chicken coop?"

He says yes and then lets the conversation drift comfortably into autopilot mode as they reminisce, explain the whole thing to Karen. There's so much that Patrick knows Dorian couldn't possibly explain about it, and he wonders if he should tell Dorian about what's been happening, about his visions. Probably not, not in front of Karen. He's asking about it now, about Zen, the stories, the mysteries they solved when they were detectives. The demigods planted the evidence. The nostalgia is bothersome. As if nothing can be significant until it becomes historical data. As if they no longer live in the present.

Lately, there is always a lot of noise in Patrick's head, ever since his fall. Never silence. Impossible to ignore, like a stereo blasting in the next room, or a television that's too loud. The noise is indescribable, like white noise, hardly a noise at all. Can try to cover it up with loud music or trying to think louder. HOW LOUD CAN I THINK? And sometimes the loud thinking can be just as frustrating as the noise. There's an ethereal kind of poetry to it, listening to the brain noise closely and asking himself what am I listening to, who is listening, what is listening, what is it that hears, is it a mind, is it my own mind, what is that?

... THE SENATOR IS REPORTED TO HAVE TAKEN AS MUCH AS A HALF-MILLION DOLLARS IN KICKBACKS FROM POST-KATRINA CONSTRUCTION PROJECTS...

They continue to eat. Dorian looks pensive.

"You know what I find fascinating when I think about the games we played as kids? They involved everybody in the neighborhood. Like when everybody in the neighborhood used to get together and play kick the can or tennis baseball. I'm really interested in community interaction. That's part of the reason we bought this house. I think we've lost the sense of community we used to have. The sense of belonging as part of a larger system—like a computer network. Besides, we might be squeezing out some puppies soon, you know."

Karen groans, stands up to get another beer from the refrigerator.

Ashley once told Patrick that everybody hears noises in their heads, but that's hard for him to believe. How then could there be people who didn't like poetry or didn't understand art? And then there are people like Dorian who think the world makes complete sense. And there are people who like the noise that their television sets make, and they must not have any noises of their own to deal with. Nirvana is silence.

Patrick lets his eyes wander to the beige carpet, beige walls, beige ceiling. The entertainment center neatly organized in the next room. The news on the television has come around full circle. Chastity Roberts, the very familiar-looking news anchor.

... A COMMUNITY IN NORTHEAST MISSISSIPPI WAS

DISTURBED TODAY . . .

Sense of belonging as part of a larger system.

"You want to take a walk around the neighborhood after dinner?"

"Sure, why not?"

"Hey, remember when we were in high school and we . . ."

Patrick chews his food and nods as Dorian continues to reminisce about days when they still lived in the present. Nostalgia annihilates the present, leaves no place for the future. Just what are we doing, he thinks, celebrating the death of the present tense in our lives? He thinks of *Dasein*, Being with a capital Bee, the all-encompassing term of the inimitable Martin H, being, being-there permanently and deliberately. This conversation is the death of *Dasein*—possibly this is what Heidegger means by the darkening of the world, the flight of the gods, the emasculation of the spirit.

Dorian gets a flashlight, and the three of them head out the door. Some of the houses are different colors; some have one floor, and others have two, but essentially, they all look the same. And all the streets have the same name. Lakeview Street. Lakeview Court. Lakeview Drive. Lakeview Circle. Lakeview Lane. In the middle of the neighborhood, the eponymous lake, actually a mosquito-scum-covered pond that's supporting a community of frogs, crickets, cicadas, fire ants, and quite possibly water moccasins. A sign says "No swimming. No Fishing."

Dorian points ahead with his flashlight.

"There's a new unit they put up down the road. The people haven't moved in yet, and there's no furniture, but everything in it is white. The floors, ceiling, walls, everything. I'm wondering if they're gonna put white carpet in it. Can you imagine?"

Karen pipes in, bubbling, "Ooh, I saw the carpet truck this morning."

"Excellent. I'm just dying to know what color this carpet is."

They come up to the empty house, and Dorian shines his flashlight in the window.

"Yeah," Dorian says, "they've got the carpet. I can't tell the color. It might be pink." Patrick follows them around the carport to the back of the house. Dorian feels around the top of the doorway. "No key. Well, the good news, sort of, is that these houses are a lot easier to get into than the older ones like ours.

Dorian hands the flashlight to Karen and takes a credit card out of his wallet. In a few seconds they're inside, and Karen is shining light across the floor. Dorian titters. "Ah, mauve. They're doing mauve and forest green. Look! The little diamonds on the kitchen floor are forest green."

In the surrounding shadows, Patrick expects to see a demigod or three, but the house is as empty as he wishes his head were. They step through each room, Dorian speculating to himself about the lives of the new owners. Patrick tunes him out, hearing only his brain noise, which descends on him like a swarm of angry yellow jackets. He says he doesn't feel well, is going to head back.

Outside, Patrick feels mocked by the buzz of the streetlights, the crickets, frogs, cicadas and the traffic on the highway beyond the tree line. He can smell the honeysuckle and the jasmine, can feel them choking the imported holly bushes and oak trees. Parasites. The crickets echo a strange Pentecostal hymn through the dry air. Unusual, he thinks, for the air to be dry in Birmingham.

In a passing window, an elderly woman leans out, mournfully sweeping soot from the window ledge—residue emitted from the nearby steel mills. She is close enough for Patrick to see her wet eyes, which she quickly hides when she notices him. After a second, she disappears into the house. She is a fleeting, sad specter.

His thoughts turn then to that lit rag whose party he crashed, and its pretty pair of editors. He wonders if that project really has the potential to keep him rooted here, if this is where he'll end up—not in the wooded suburbs, but Birmingham—with all its

bedraggled history laid out like a cadaver for any and all to view.
Like any town, he supposes Lyonness has a history too, although
nobody ever bothered to tell him what it was.

Chapter 8

Rebecca looks through the backlog of submissions, decides to break the monotony by calling the office to check messages. There is one: "Hi. This is Patrick Alexander. I wondered if we could have coffee sometime and talk about the magazine. I don't have a phone where you can call me back, but if you want to meet, I'll be at The Booksmith tonight between seven and nine. If you can meet me, fine. I'll be there regardless. Bye."

She spends a few seconds wondering who Patrick Alexander is before she remembers the man from the party. It sounds like it could be his voice, that rural twang and a roughness from smoking cigarettes. The Entity. An Entity. Whatever. She plays back the message. Patrick Alexander. What the hell is that about?

Between seven and nine. It's just past seven now.

After pouring a can of vegetable soup into a 1-quart sauce pan, she turns on the radio. The aria is familiar to her, but she can't quite place it, hums along tentatively. She's pretty sure it's by Wagner. A basso slowly sings *Durch Mitleid wissend der reine Tor; harre sein, den ich erkor* . . . After she has stirred the soup for a minute, she collects together two pieces of white bread, a slice of American cheese, and a pat of butter, and she assembles them in a small frying pan.

The music fades away with airy voices *Durch Mitleid wissend, der reine Tor* . . . , and a news announcement comes on. *The senator from Mississippi who was indicted yesterday for* . . . She changes the station, humming the romantic violin piece to drown out the static. . . . *-lores Stokes of Birmingham was found dead today in* . . . She turns it back. . . . *Bronson has disappeared. Authorities say he was heading* . . . She turns the radio off.

By then, her sandwich is ready, and her soup is warm. She sits down with her meal and begins to browse through the magazine submissions. Gradually, she puts the manuscripts in stacks, making them less intimidating. After a while, she yawns and thinks why bother? It's doomed anyway. She looks up at her clock—half past seven. She supposes she could use a cup of coffee. She gets her purse and walks down to The Booksmith, a hybrid bookstore and coffeehouse a few blocks from her apartment.

She apparently just missed a poetry reading, so it's more crowded than usual. A college-age girl, an employee of the bookstore, walks around with a silver tray of hors d'oeuvres. Another is giving out little cups of wine. The poet, a white bearded academic named Lance Wood, whom she knows all too well, stands by the door surrounded by a small throng of female students. He waves at her and gives her a sly wink.

She waves back meekly and slips by. At a table in the corner, a homely girl appears to be writing the great American novel. At another table, a group of young artist types in full-on black turtleneck regalia speak loudly about expatriation and bondage. Several more conservative-looking people linger in the spaces between bookshelves, possibly hiding from their spouses or from their friends.

From the farthest corner table, Patrick flags her down. She recognizes his hair from across the room, sticking up like a bush of monkey grass. He's smoking a cigarette. She signals to him that she'll be right there and goes to the counter to get a cup of coffee. The woman behind the counter misunderstands her and thinks she ordered a piece of chocolate pound cake. She takes the cake and goes over to Patrick's table where he reaches out for her hand. "Hi. You got my message. How are you?"

"Bored as hell, and by the way, that's the only reason I'm here. Yourself?"

"All right, I guess. I have some stuff for you." He hands her a folder. She looks in, and it looks like some poems. More crap to read, she thinks. No thanks. "That's not a submission. It's just for you, so you can, you know, get to know me better."

"I'll take a look at it later," she says. Tell me something about yourself."

"Like what?"

"Like what's the deal with the name thing?" He looks puzzled. "You left your name on the answering machine message, but you wouldn't tell it to me the other day."

"You didn't ask. I'd have told you if you'd asked. I don't like to leave any concrete evidence of myself lying around unless I want it to mean something. It's a way of keeping a step ahead of the system, to keep from being reduced to a name in a filing cabinet or on someone's computer."

He could have said that the other day, she thinks, but she would have thought it was terribly corny. "That's terribly corny."

"Yeah, I know."

The poet and his entourage come into the coffeehouse area. They are followed by the hors d'oeuvres girl and the wine girl. The poet signs a copy of his book for one of the students as he walks, and he accidentally bumps his hip on the coffee counter. As he grimaces and checks his wound, one of the students asks if he's bleeding.

A drunken dwarf in a red tuxedo follows closely behind yelling to them, "He's no novelist. He's a novelizationist!"

Rebecca turns her attention back to Patrick. He's wearing a ridiculous grin. "I do have some ideas about the magazine," he says.

"You know, I don't know if I actually want to hear them."

"Why'd you come here then?"

"I don't know. I guess . . . Well, okay . . . We can talk about that. It's just that I'm getting really tired of what I've been doing with the magazine, and I have this overwhelming sensation that it's beyond help. We keep dealing with the same little clique of artists, some of whom are really good, but it's always the same old stuff. We're not getting the community support we used to have, and so it's getting difficult to sell ads, and on top of that, my co-editor is moving to Florida for God's sake in a few weeks."

"What for? Is she retiring?"

"Haha. She's going to graduate school, an M.F.A. in theatre or something . . . Anyway, what have you got?"

"Well look. I don't have much experience, but I read a lot, and I think you guys are on the right track, but the approach is too timid. I think you can go more avant-garde, more subversive . . ."

As he continues talking about his theories about art and literature—which strike her, by the way, as utter bullshit—the words disappear, but his face becomes plastic with excitement as he pontificates in his almost old-world Southern accent. For a moment, she wants to kiss him, but then she remembers that she really doesn't like him. She nods and tries not to yawn, and waits for him to conclude his thesis. Then it's her turn again. "Where are you from?" she says.

"A little town in Mississippi called Lyonness."

"I'm from Jackson, but I never heard of Lyonness. What's it near?"

"It's off U.S. 82, just west of the Alabama state line."

She considers this a moment, trying to imagine what life would be like for an artistic, liberal-minded person there in Lyonness, Mississippi. Probably not that much different from Jackson. Isolated, lonely. No doubt, it's full of the same kind of blustery born-agains and philistines. She doesn't want to talk about Mississippi, though and decides to get back down to business. "Alright. What's your schedule like over the next couple of weeks?"

"At the moment, it's completely open. Unless I find a job. I'm thinking about applying here. I like this place."

"Well, call me in a couple of days, and I'll give you a stack of things to read. That way we'll have something more concrete to talk about." She wraps the piece of cake in a napkin and puts it in her pocket. She gets up to leave, and he walks her out.

"Saturday night, some friends of mine are playing at this party." He hands her a card. She hands it back to him.

"Yeah, I already have one of these."

His face lights up. "Right on. Maybe I'll see you there. Do you need a ride anywhere?" He gestures toward a red motorcycle parked in front of the store.

"No thanks. I live just down the street from here. I can walk. Call me in a couple of days, okay?"

He goes back inside. As she walks past the open green park between the bookstore and her apartment building, Rebecca watches a kid run across the grass flying a kite. Parents sit at a nearby table watching approvingly as the kite soars above like a giant white bird. A wild goose perhaps.

Chapter 9

Patrick accompanies Dorian on his morning walk, and Dorian audibly inhales a healthy bouquet of August air. "Breathe," he says. "It's free."

A hot wind creeps across the pavement. Patrick takes a strained breath, and his nose flutters. He coughs, spits.

"Your lungs are full of garbage, Patrick. You can't live like this."

"I'm alright. It's just my allergies."

"And the cigarettes, and the drinking, and the pot . . ."

"Thanks, mom. I'll keep that in mind. And I'm running pretty low on pot. Know where I can . . ." The question is interrupted by Dorian's disapproving leer.

On the other side of the street, cars are lined up all the way down the block. Patrick stops to watch as women in black dresses, some crying, carry platters inside the house. Men in dark suits stand around with their hands in their pockets. A gray-haired priest steps out of one of the cars carrying a book under his arm.

Jesus, Patrick thinks. Same house where he saw that strange, crying woman. A fleeting moment, but he felt a certain sorrow for her then, such as he hadn't felt in a long while. "What is the meaning of this?" Not what he meant to say.

Dorian, who has kept walking, suddenly seems to notice Patrick's pause and returns. "What?"

"What's going on over there?

"You didn't hear about this on the news last night? You really are out of it. You were sitting right there when they talked about it."

"Well, what was it?"

"I'm getting to it. She killed herself . . . three days ago. Her name was Delores somethingorother. "

"Three days ago? Tuesday?"

Patrick is trying to think if that was the same night he saw the woman in the window. He wants to say, although I never knew you, I grieve your death, wants to say it in Latin to make it sound more official, but he doesn't know any Latin. Dorian doesn't answer his question.

"Herb, the next door neighbor, told me that she cut out her own heart, although I find that pretty hard to believe. I don't know why people feel the need to make up stuff like that. Anyway, they found her the other day. She was an old woman, old as God. Herb used to run errands for her sometimes, get her groceries and stuff. I never met her, myself."

They walk back toward the house.

Patrick is silent all through breakfast. His sinuses throbbing, he wanders to the hallway bathroom and stares in the mirror. He stares intently into his own eyes, trying to follow the network of signs that keep flashing in his mind. Martians. Monkeys. Lizards. Disturbed. Tree. Body. Community. Cut out her own heart.

With his head noise pounding now with the weight of an unconfessed sin, he tries, really tries for a moment to see, to feel connected to something. He looks into his own eyes for signs of anything—Ashley or Rebecca maybe—but there's nothing. Maybe he's in over his head with that literary magazine. It excited him because there's really nothing like that in Lyonness. But ultimately, it would probably just end up being another job he'd resent having to do. In the mirror, he sees Harold slink up behind him, hoarsely whispering something unintelligible. He hears Dorian call out a hasty goodbye as he leaves for work. Karen has already been gone for a couple of hours.

Patrick follows the lizard to the master bedroom. On the dresser, there are pictures from Dorian and Karen's wedding in New Orleans a couple of years earlier. He can see himself in the corner of a candid shot from the reception, eyelids heavy from drink. Ashley is there too, somewhere in the throngs.

The room is meticulous, bed made up, frilly pillow shams. Randomly, he opens a drawer. Dorian's tee shirts are neatly folded and stacked in three equal piles. In another, just some of Karen's bras and panties. He decides to stop snooping before he finds anything interesting.

Harold is gone.

Passing through the kitchen, he notices another snapshot on the refrigerator, the four of them one New Year's Eve a couple of years ago. They're all wearing glittery party hats and grinning at the camera, arm in arm. He snatches it down and then retreats to his room, putting the photo in his backpack.

He paces back and forth a few times, then lies back on the bed and masturbates. Afterwards, he smokes the dregs of the weed he has left in his bag. Seeds and stems. Then, finally, oblivion.

Chapter 10

This is the land created by a childgod.

Rebecca's reading the material Patrick gave her at the Booksmith, and, as she feared, it's just a bunch of bad poetry. Really bad. A lot of abstract, self-important metaphysical stuff about demigods and personal mythic history. Boring. And underneath all the heady, purple language, it doesn't seem to mean much, as far as she can tell. But he has presence, a kind of magnetism. She can't stop thinking about him. She wants to like the poems, to have that indiscriminate taste of a schoolgirl crush. That would bring a bit of excitement into her life at least, but she feels like she's just too jaded.

The card he gave her is still on her dresser. She's heard of the band, and she hasn't heard much good about them, but what the hell? It's been a while since she went out to see live music, and she doesn't have any other plans.

The map takes her a few miles outside of town, near Montevallo. She's been to parties in that area before. There's a small liberal arts college there, which gives it a vibrant, esoteric youth culture.

A hand-written posterboard sign on the side of the road points her down a dirt road, past a field of goats, and finally to an expansive field littered with cars and people drinking beer from plastic cups. Still inside her car, she hears the rumble of drums coming from inside the nearby barn. She can see a pale, red glow spilling out from the inside into a fenced-in area of the yard. She parks, turning around in case a quick getaway becomes necessary, takes a deep breath, and walks up to the gate.

An emaciated, shirtless imp with pierced nipples and green hair holds up three fingers, representing dollars. Cheap. She gives him the money, and he draws an x-eyed smiley face on the back of her hand with a black marker.

The inside smells like sweat and beer, not much like a barn. It doesn't really look like a barn on the inside either. It's been gutted and divided into multiple rooms. The walls are finished and decorated with abstract posters. There's carpet. It seems to have been renovated specifically to be a venue, or perhaps it's Danny Brewer's bachelor pad.

The band, seemingly in the middle of some kind of tribal percussion piece, is set up at the back of a large front room. Also on the stage are two people, a man and a woman, naked but covered from head to foot with iridescent body paint, dancing in the flickering light of a film projector. It's difficult to tell what the images on the screen are, but it strikes her as medical, possibly an educational film about the human digestive system. The dancers squirm and wiggle through the body like chunks of food being swallowed and ingested. In front of the band, a crowd of people is bound together by their perspiration. The throng moves slowly from side to side as if moved by gargantuan masticating jaws.

The drum solo seems to go on endlessly, and she decides to search for the promised keg. As she makes her way around the edge of the crowd, an ecstatic hippie is excreted from the populous beast. "The Expletives know, man. They just know."

"Um, that's great. Do you know where the beer is?"

He points to a doorway near the stage, on the other side of the dancing crowd. Once again, she takes a deep breath, but this time she inhales a cloud of toxic smoke, which makes her cough. She squeezes herself through the wet corpuscles of the beast, slipping out at the other end with only a few small bruises. Just as she passes in front of a p.a. speaker, the band starts playing again, loudly. Another body is regurgitated from the pit, knocking her over face first into the wall with his rear end. She turns around to find that it had been the bony buns of Patrick.

He promptly apologizes and leads her to a room slightly further from the noise and crowd. She is limping, leaning on his shoulder. Patrick clears a space for her among a group of stoners sitting on a sofa, announcing that there's been an injury. He asks if she needs anything.

"Twisted my ankle I think."

He disappears briefly, reappears with a clump of ice, presumably from one of the beer coolers, wrapped in his shirt. She notices that he has a lot of freckles on his chest and large crimson birthmarks on his arms. He says something, which she thinks is an offer to make her dinner sometime to compensate for her injuries.

"What?"

The band is still so loud, she has to shout to talk to him. He repeats the proposal.

"Is that a threat?"

"I'm an excellent cook."

"I'll think about it. In the meantime, can you get me a beer?"

He brings her beer, sits on the sofa next to her. She grasps for something to say to him. In a lull between songs, she thinks of the packet he gave her.

"I read your poetry. I don't know what it means."

"It doesn't mean anything."

"I don't think I like it."

"Fair enough."

She looks at him, searching his face for signs that she's hurt his feelings, if he has any. He seems sincere in his antipathy, and she finds this oddly appealing. The noise of the party is already starting to get to her. She massages her temples.

"Look, if you aren't into this party, we could go hang out at my place. It's nearby."

Without thinking it over, she agrees to this. Her ankle seems to be okay now, so she follows him outside to her car.

"I'll go get my motorcycle, and you can follow me there."

"Don't go too fast. It's hard to see out here."

Rebecca gets in the car and waits for him to come into view. She isn't given to premonitions, at least not positive ones, but she has an odd, comforting sensation that this is all leading to something that might turn out to be interesting.

In a few moments, she hears the buzz of the motorcycle pulling up next to her. He gives a signal and then moves forward. She follows him about half a mile down the nearest paved road and then turns off into a suburban development called Lakeview. When they arrive there, she's more than a little shocked at the bland surroundings. Not at all what she would have pictured.

"You live here?"

"Temporarily. I'm staying with friends until I find my own place. They're still out, probably at the party."

He gets her a glass of water and puts some music on. They chat briefly about how he and his roommates have known the guys in that band since they were kids. He mentions an ex-wife in Mississippi and then becomes suddenly quiet.

"Are you okay?"

"Yeah. Sorry. I didn't mean to bring that up."

"It's over, right? You've moved on."

"Yeah."

A few moments later, they kiss, and an ephemeral comfort is called into existence like one of those demigods he talks about in his poems. But when he finally takes her into his stark bedroom, and they have sex, the mundane novelty of holding someone inside her body seems more annoying than thrilling, and she is even struck by a vague emotion that is almost like guilt but with less direction. His skin is rough, and his hands and arms appear to be swollen and red. She goes on with it, trying to make the best of it, but she feels more like she's being bitten by a mosquito than being fucked.

The sound of sirens outside helps her to not think. She finally comes, but at that point of release, she becomes nothingness. She lies afterward with a warm angry sensation that is not directed at Patrick or at herself, but at the act, the rewardless urge. She feels like they have traded souls, that she is now the one acting serious and ridiculous. He is far less brooding. He falls asleep quickly, holding her mechanically. She stays, feeling that her uneasiness is irrational, knowing that casual sex has always made her feel this way.

Chapter 11

Patrick wakes up in the early morning. It's still dark out, and Rebecca sleeps soundly. Slowly and silently, he gets up and rummages through his back pack for a mostly-empty fifth of whiskey he liberated from the party the night before. He grabs the neck of the bottle like the hilt of a sword and goes out.

Outside, the air is hot. Most of the cars are gone from in front of the dead woman's house.

Patrick comes to the end of the developed area of the neighborhood and enters the waste forest. Plastic jugs and empty beer bottles settle among the pond weeds. The interstate buzzes over his head. From the dry leaves to his right he hears a rustling. The animal looks up at him briefly with pink eyes then retreats into the woods. It looks like a doe, an albino. Taking another swig of his whiskey, he follows.

Before long, the sun is starting to come up. He doesn't see the doe anywhere. The woods are sparse, only a few small trees, the roots of which stick out of the ground like so many uncovered bones in a washed out graveyard. Dogwood and birch slowly being strangled by kudzu. Nothing big like a pine tree. Nothing like the mythic South.

Quite a farce this South where we wear the relics of our maiden history on our sleeves as his father used to say during the commercials, Son, the only good thing about the South is that it's better than anywhere else. Sound observations from the man who called him "nigger" when his skin got brown from the summer sun. Maybe he should try New York for a while, or California. He can't quite imagine it though, being a Southern boy through and through.

Everything always seems to come back to heritage. Family tree of knowledge. Where does the tree fit in? Can it fit into your mind? Is a mind something that things can fit into? Things like trees? His father never answered questions like that. He rarely answered even questions like what time is it. No sense that time was passing or even that there was an orderly pattern to the various images that flashed before him on the television that he had built with his own hands during an earlier golden era. Gripping the bamboo pole that he used to push the buttons from the sofa, his remote control he said, he jumped from scene to scene with no apparent (or at least no consistent) criteria for remaining on or changing a station. The only cause and effect was the force of the bamboo pole against the plastic, which made the images change. Not like a mind.

Patrick feels a reassuring hand touch his shoulder from behind, and in his haziness he feels it is his father's hand. But when he turns around, he sees Senator Bronson. The pocked nose of the senator is about six inches away. His grey yellow hair, though short and thin, stands on end like the wisping swab of a disturbed Q-tip, as if God had pulled this senator out of a blue cardboard box, dipped him in alcohol, and cleaned His omnipotent ear. Bronson's lips are pursed, almost pouting, and his eyes are opened wide, paralyzed with fear. Patrick recognizes the senator even in his rags, and he tries to think of something to say.

"Oh, shit." He takes the bottle out of his pocket. "I don't have any whiskey left."

The senator looks relieved and motions for Patrick to follow him. Cautiously a few paces behind, Patrick follows Bronson into a denser section of the woods. They come to a clearing and Bronson brings out all manner of breads, potato chips, canned vegetables, fried chicken, and drinks from a trunk that he had hidden in the bushes. Bronson hands Patrick a fresh pint of whiskey, a more expensive brand than he would ever buy. "Where'd you get all this?"

"Friends."

"They'll give you food, but they won't put you up for the night?"

"That's right." He takes a drink. "Had a place to stay until the other night, an aunt who lives in one of those houses. She's got relatives there now, and I can't stay, so I'm camping out 'til they're gone."

"You don't get along with the rest of the relatives?"

"Now listen here. What're you doing out here in the middle of the night? Don't you know there're dangerous people in the woods at night?"

"What makes you think I'm not one of them?"

"Hell, a scrawny kid like you? I could kick your ass in a heartbeat. You should eat something."

He hands Patrick a leg of fried chicken and then resumes his drinking.

"Why'd you reach out for me earlier? I'd think you'd be hiding. A lot of people are looking for you."

"I thought you were somebody else. Young man my aunt's been sending . . . Quit asking me questions. You make me nervous."

They sit for a long time in silence, drinking and eating. Bronson sits cross-legged on the ground and seems engrossed in his sitting. A car roars down the highway, nearby but out of sight. Bronson lights a small fire, which casts a strange light on the surrounding trees. He begins to cook some beans over the fire. Slightly drunk and very tired, Patrick intensely watches the shadows. Shadows always remind him of women the way they remind small children of monsters. A particular shadow takes shape, walks as lightly as wind around the fire with arms outstretched carrying something. She comes closer hovering behind Bronson's back. Her hair falls in golden curls over her shoulders like Ashley's. Covered from head to toe in a white silk gown, her face is hidden. Patrick can see that she is holding a large chalice, plated with gold and encrusted in jewels. As she hovers closer she lowers the chalice so that Patrick can see a human heart beating, dripping with blood, inside of the cup. The cup overflows and the blood sizzles as it drips into the fire.

"Delores."

"Wha?" Bronson takes the beans off the fire. They've started to boil over. "Must have dozed off."

"I just had a vision."

"Here. Eat some beans," Bronson says. "They're good for your heart. The more you eat 'em, the more you like 'em."

"Look. I gotta go. I was just reminded of something I have to do. Thanks for everything. This was quite enlightening. Good night."

Bronson looks up at him, smiling.

"You want to know something?"

"No thanks. I know too much already."

"Godspeed."

Rebecca wakes up the next morning with Patrick's hand on her knee. He's sitting up on the edge of the bed, looking at her seriously, the way he seemed at the party where she first met him. "I have to leave here," he says. "I feel like I've done all I can here."

"What are you talking about? What about the magazine? You said that we need you."

"Yeah, um. I guess I was wrong about that. Anyway, I told you my ideas. I gave you my opinion for what it's worth. If it appeals to you, use it. If not, think of something else."

"And what about me?"

"You're a big girl."

"I don't understand. Where are you going?"

Why does she care, she thinks. It was a one-night stand, a mistake. He seems to consider the question for a few moments before answering. "I don't know. I need to find something, and this morning it became apparent to me that I'm not going to find it here."

"Fuck you."

She sits in silence while he stuffs clothes in an old backpack. She begins putting on her own clothes, wondering who the hell he thinks he is.

"Um, not that it's really my business, but wouldn't it make more sense to stay here until you have a better plan than just wandering off?"

"Look. I can't give you a logical explanation. I have to go. That's what I do. "

"It's what you do? What kind of crap is that?"

Patrick mounts the overfilled backpack on his shoulders. "Oh, and there's another thing. I've accumulated a lot of clothes here somehow. It's more than I can carry, so I want you to have them. Do whatever you want with them. I'm leaving now."

"Right now?"

She watches him walk out the door. She stands there a moment in her underwear and shirt, confused, pissed off. Then she lies back down on the bed, staring at the ceiling for what seems like an hour.

It was a mistake, sure, but how can she make the best of it? She looks in the closet at the wardrobe he left behind—mainly thrift store and Army surplus fare, a couple of hats. She puts on one of the hats, a black fedora with a white band, and walks into the living room in search of a mirror.

A tall, darkly tanned girl walks out of the other bedroom, wearing a bathrobe and yawning.

"Oh, hello. I'm Karen. You must be Patrick's guest from last night."

"Yes, my name is Rebecca. Rebecca Halley."

She becomes fidgety. How is she going to explain where Patrick is? Did Patrick's roommates know that something like this could happen? Karen starts grinding some coffee beans. "Were y'all still there when the fire started?"

"No. What happened?"

"Apparently, something in the, uh, what do you call it . . . the microphone system."

"The p.a.?"

"Right, the p.a. caught on fire, and before we knew it, the flames were everywhere. You can imagine once it got near all that alcohol it was really blazing. The place burned to the ground. It was wild."

She considers for a moment what her response is supposed to be. It sounds grim, but it's hard to get her head around it, considering all she's been though this morning. "Um, was anybody hurt? "

"A couple of people, but nothing serious. Is Patrick still asleep?" A little nervously, Rebecca shrugs, shakes her head no. Karen's face slowly transforms as she puzzles this scenario together. "Oh, God . . . He just . . . wandered off didn't he? Look, sugar, don't imagine this has anything to do with you. It isn't your fault at all. It's completely normal behavior for Patrick. He's crazy. Did he say anything else?"

"He said he wanted me to have all his clothes."

"Okaaaaaaay. Time for Dorian to get up."

Karen disappears back in to the bedroom, and Rebecca helps herself to a cup of coffee. After a few minutes, Dorian stumbles out mumbling. He's wearing a full set of plaid pajamas, which she can't help but find adorable, which is also the word that came to mind when she first heard Karen speak.

"Now what has that fool gone and done?"

"I don't know . . . You know him better than I do. He's your friend. Deal with it. Ask her."

"Hello, I'm Dorian, Patrick's, um, friend. Now, did he happen to say anything about Ashley, his wife."

"Wife? He told me ex-wife."

"It varies. What did he say?"

Rebecca recaps for him.

"Well, goddamn. It's nice to meet you just the same. Want some breakfast?"

Chapter 12

This is the land created by a childgod, and in this land an absurd bond exists between the entities that inhabit it—a bittersweet cocktail of security, convenience and poetry.

Monkeyman sits in lotus position on the handlebars, not obstructing Patrick's view because he is translucent. He is calm and serious as he lectures. "We sometimes call this absurdity love, and sometimes when we are feeling more esoteric we call it enlightenment, represented by the image of the Buddha. When philosophers ask what is enlightenment and esoterics ask what is the Buddha, they ask the same question. All the universe is wind and sweat, rock and rain. The absurdity lies within us, within our homes, in the way we divide up the world into the us and the not us. There really should be no distinction."

The droning hum of the motorcycle, like the om of the Eastern ascetics, contains many layers of tones, of words, of stories. Patrick feels light-headed. He speeds up the interstate aimlessly, trying to organize his thoughts into something that rings of epiphany.

He stops to refuel his body and his bike at a truck stop. Everywhere he sees the same desperate look. When he goes into the shit-stained bathrooms to piss in tobacco-clogged toilets, he sees the same despair in his own foggy reflection. There's a crumpled newspaper wedged in the corner of the booth where he sits in the truck stop restaurant, and he pulls it out as he sips his coffee, shovels home fries down his throat.

Monkeyman, on the back of his seat reading over Patrick's shoulder, suddenly starts screeching and points out a small article in the international news section. An outbreak of the black plague in India. The land of the Buddha. The same disease that almost wiped out the medieval world, a world that worshipped such relics as the holy grail. The hero of the East—Buddha. The hero of the West—Christ, no King Arthur. Christ was a hero for the world. But all three represent an unseen power at work in the universe.

He must be mumbling this to himself when, after paying his bill, he walks his bike around to the back to check the air in the tires. A sickly looking white boy, maybe 16 or 17, in tight red shorts, approaches him. His short black hair sticks up on one side as if he had been sleeping. In his eyes, Patrick feels like he sees the dreams of a distracted sleep still holding him prisoner. The boy extends a bruised and withered arm. "You wanna joust?"

His words fall heavily like a polluted cloud. Patrick considers the meaning of this, how to respond. He eyes the dry red sores around the boy's mouth, the sticky drop of snot slowly leaking from his nostril. "No. Thanks anyway."

He starts his motorcycle. The boy takes a butterfly knife from the back of his pants. "Then give me your jacket."

"Fuck off." Patrick easily kicks the boy over as he rides away.

Knocking him down is like kicking a stuffed animal. As he rides away, he looks back and sees that the kid is laughing—and puking.

He gets back on the interstate, heading North through a light rainfall, toward the hills of the lower Appalachians. He listens to the om of the motor between his legs. The monkey continues his lecture. "Humanity's historical *Dasein*, in Martin H.'s language, depends greatly on its perspective of nothingness (what the Japanese call *ku* or 'the sky's emptiness'). In metaphysics, this nothingness is contrasted with essents, things that are. What Heidegger said was that this 'nothingness' is not just an empty set as in logic, but rather it has an essential role in defining the essence of being. If 'nothingness' were an empty set, then 'being' would be merely a hollow and meaningless term. The decay of spirituality in the West is largely the result of our losing touch with the true meaning of 'being' which is the essence of Being in the broader sense. Enlightenment, in the Eastern sense, is traditionally associated with something like 'becoming one' with the universe. Part of this is realizing the true nature of nothingness, obliterating the boundary line between the I and the not I, between the essent and the nothing. The search for enlightenment, in the Buddhist sense, is easily comparable to the search for salvation in the Christian sense, and, taking a more Gnostic or mystical approach, comparable to the search for the Holy Grail. So there. They all have the same disease. The plague strikes all. Wind and sweat rock and rain."

When Patrick responds aloud, his voice reverberates inside the motorcycle helmet. "OK, so what does that mean for me? And more importantly, where the hell am I going?"

Monkeyman answers with silence.

Chapter 13

Water. A mouse-eared molecule, not unlike the public face of a certain multinational entertainment conglomerate. It's fitting that those dream developers, whether by accident or design, picked a symbol that so closely represents one of the primary conditions for life. Pointy-headed men in white lab coats say that where there is water, there is life, so they look for water on distant moons, distant planets, where the relics of some bacteria or fishy organism may lie in wait for discovery.

Long ago, or not so long ago, we were the fish. The fish grew legs and lungs and language. Humans gathered on the water's edge, wherever there was an edge of water to gather upon, and soon enough began civilization by eating their own history until they no longer believed it. But the ancientness of it, the ritual of it, remains. It remains as the rustic man in his early 50s, Pell Ragnell, in the obligatory rural Alabama mufti of denim overalls and

John Deere baseball cap, pours gasoline into the tank of his outboard motor at the edge of a small, rustic lakeside pier.

Pell didn't catch anything this morning, and also his stomach was feeling woozy. He had the runs for a little while earlier, but he's feeling a bit better now. Generally, Pell hasn't been feeling too well lately, what with these stomach problems and a rash on his arms and chest. But he and his boarders need something for supper, and anyway, he can't stand hanging around the house with all of them lolling about in the parlor. He tends to keep to himself, either in his workshop or in the kitchen, lets Clara keep the tenants entertained. He knows a couple of shady spots where he can resume his vocation without taking too much of a beating from the sun.

Wilhelmina, the family's pet potbelly pig, rushes around the corner to see him off. He rubs Wilhelmina on the head, finds a stick on the ground and throws it into the distance for her to chase. That's one good pig, he thinks.

He's grateful that Clara was there to take over the place when his parents passed on. He doesn't have a head for business, but Clara has it all under control, leaving him to his hobbies, which keep him occupied.

From the house to his back, a screen door squeaks open. Clara is standing in the doorway with a sheet of paper in her hand.

"Pell, you're still here. Good. I just got an email from Victoria. I printed it out for you. 'God most of the classes I wanted . . .' One would think that someone who is currently a magazine editor and about to enter graduate studies would check her spelling. 'Got most of the classes I wanted. I'm going to take Russian in addition to my acting classes. I leave in two weeks. Give Wilhelmina a kiss for me. Love you. Vic.'"

"That's it?"

"That's it."

She hands him the sheet of paper, and he folds it into his

shirt pocket. Pell steps carefully into the boat. Wilhelmina comes running down the pier, makes a plaintive snorting sound.

"Okay Willie, come on."

He helps the pig into the stern of the vessel, starts the engine and sets out. He waves to Clara as she fades away behind the brushwood. "Careful out there, Pell," she calls.

That daughter of his is a miracle. After a piece of shrapnel hit near his groin in the Mekong Delta, he didn't think he'd ever have children. Worst thing is that he walks with a slight limp. He was lucky. Always has been. Wonder what possessed her to take Russian. Is she turning into a commie down there in the big city? Surely she has her reasons.

As he comes out of the narrow tributary into the open lake, he cuts the motor and drifts, looking to see if there's anybody else on the water but sees no one. He turns on a small radio and hears the end of a news story about that cousin of his, the senator. Second cousin once removed, to be precise. Surprised he hasn't shown up here looking for a place to hide out. He used to visit once or twice a year to fish or hunt in the area. Sometimes brought a few cronies with him.

After Pell switches off the radio, he hears the raspy rattle of a kingfisher in the air. Sure enough, a blue-gray blur swoops down not ten feet from his boat and comes up with a small fish in its bill then alights on a tree branch at the edge of the lake to swallow its meal. Willie watches the bird intently, apparently as fascinated as Pell is, if not more.

Soon after that, a shadow descends onto the lake—a hawk. The kingfisher dives straight into the water. Meanwhile the hawk completes his arc, sees nothing of interest to him, and disappears back into the wood before the kingfisher re-emerges.

Pell figures all the bird activity has probably scared most of the fish away from this part of the lake and motors on to a more secluded area across the way.

❧

On the highway, there's a sign for boat rentals, so Patrick knows there's water nearby, and the afternoon has gotten increasingly hot. He takes the next exit, winds down a country road, hoping to find a swimming hole or some other oasis. Following this road, he eventually happens upon a lake, parks his motorcycle and strips down. A quick dip in the cold water revives his energies but offers him no relief from despair. He now just feels more vigorously desperate.

After swimming around aimlessly for a couple of minutes, he floats on his back, eyes closed, sunlight dancing over his eyelids. Ashley comes to mind, an image of her alone, pacing the cheap treadmill that she bought from the church bazaar a few years ago. He always thought it was crazy to walk like that for an hour or more and not ever get anywhere. The odometer on it was broken anyway, so she never knew how far she'd gone even. He would have liked to have at least known that.

She's better off without him. They've both known it for a long time, and they clung together largely because they were both afraid to go it alone in the big scary world.

It's been a couple of months now since he left Lyonness, and it seems much longer. He's never stayed away for this long. Still, he's not thinking of going back. But then again, he did just now think about it, even if it was in the negative. Trying to relax his spastic brain, he attempts to imagine a void, a black hole to suck out all the clatter and clutter from his thoughts. This works for about a second, and then he pictures Harold, enflamed by a crimson corona. He can almost sense the lizard swimming in the shallows underneath him, slithering like an eel. He gets an erection just for a few seconds as his thoughts then turn to the events of the night before—it goes away when he begins to think about the morning after, this morning. Did he make a mistake, leaving Rebecca in the lurch like that? She must be pretty freaked out . . . but she'll get over it. He doesn't know anything about running a magazine, and she'd have found him out eventually.

He wades back to shore and dresses. Just as he pulls his pants on, he hears the engine of an approaching boat. After a few seconds, the boat rounds a corner and comes into view. The driver, a rusty-haired older man with a sunburned receding hairline and a white and brown pig by his side, slows down, coming toward Patrick. As the boat gets within speaking distance, the driver turns off the motor. "I see you found my little spot."

"Found it by accident, I guess."

"That's the only way to find it. Care to stick around a while and fish? Just happens I've got an extra pole. I'd appreciate the company, and you can keep what you catch."

Patrick's never been fishing in his life. That's something kids usually learn from their fathers. He realizes that the reason the man looks familiar is because he has the same ruddy, stained skin as his own, probably from spending too much time in a fishing boat in the sun. "No thanks. Fishing isn't really my thing."

"Just as well. A bit dry today anyway."

"Do you know of a place nearby where I can stay for a couple of days?"

"Sure do." The fisherman and his wife run a boarding house nearby, and the man proceeds to give him convoluted directions, which Patrick eventually understands. He thanks the man, whose name is Pell Ragnell, and gets back on his motorcycle. Winding through a maze of red clay roads, shrouded by splendorous pine trees, he is vigilant for the subtle landmarks he's been told to find.

It takes him almost half an hour, but he finds it—a large, two-story antebellum with four high round columns up front. The lake is just visible on the horizon behind it. A weather-battered sign, nearly hidden by weeds, indicates in romantic script that the name of the place is "Ragnell Oaks Plantation." The house seems sorely in need of a paint job, and the two eponymous oaks that frame the house on either side are strangely barren. For being so near a body of water, the flora all around seem dry and dead, a bone yard of leafless trees and shrubs, brown pine needles and dusty dirt. A variety of bird feeders populate the front yard, but there are no birds. Across the street, there's a fenced-in field, a bit greener but still rather arid, where a couple of thin goats and hens meander.

He parks his bike in a dirt driveway on the east side of the house. There's a ramp next to the steps going up to the porch and a plastic bucket of what looks like Cheerios next to the door. There are a couple of rotted out floorboards near the edge of the porch, over which he carefully steps. With some reservation, he sets down his backpack and knocks on the door. A middle-aged woman, plump with short oily blonde hair and bifocals, answers.

"Can I help you?"

"Yes'm. I believe I met your husband on the lake a short while ago, and he mentioned there may be a room for rent here. I'm looking for a place to stay for two or three days."

"I got a room available. The rent is $100 a week or $20 a night. That includes a bed and meals. I grow corn, collards, and cabbage in the garden. We've also got fresh eggs and goat's milk. You alright with goat's milk?"

"Sure."

"And we eat a lot of fish when we catch any. You like fish?"

"Yes. That sounds fine."

Patrick wonders where that garden could be—can't figure how anything could grow in the soil he saw out front. There must be more fertile land somewhere around here. Anyway, he already feels his life digressing, thoughts slowed down considerably, which is what he needs. He decides to stay here a few days, maybe a couple of weeks and then head somewhere else. He has a couple hundred dollars left. He becomes aware that his thoughts have shifted from the spiritual to the mundane, and this is something of a relief also.

Patrick grabs his backpack and enters a large room, sparsely decorated with country knickknacks. A round dining table dominates the center of the room. The woman introduces herself as Clara Ragnell. Patrick introduces himself as well. Her voice is flat, matter of fact, somewhere between an actress bored with her lines and a military officer assigning a drill.

"We don't ask too many questions around here. Your business is your business. This is where we eat. I've got five tenants when we're full. My husband Pell and I run the house. The kitchen is through there, and the rooms are upstairs. I'll show you to yours."

She swings open a kiddy gate, and silently, they go up the stairs. The rooms are simple, bare and small, each containing a single bed, a small dresser, an alarm clock, and a lamp on a nightstand.

"There are two bathrooms with showers, one on each end of the hall. There's a third bathroom downstairs. We have a washing machine and dryer downstairs by the kitchen. You do your own laundry. If you have your own food, you're welcome to cook it. Otherwise, you eat what I cook. We'll provide you with two towels and a set of sheets, which you will be responsible for washing. If you don't keep the room neat, or if you don't get along with the other tenants, you will be evicted on the spot. You pay for each night in advance. You may pay as much in advance as you like. Everything sound okay?"

"Yes, fine." He hands her twenty dollars.

"Okay, then I'll leave you then. Dinner is at six-thirty. If you can't make it to a meal, let me know in advance so I'll know how much to cook. I don't like to waste food. Will we see you at dinner?"

"Yes, ma'am."

She nods and exits.

Secure in his quarters, he digs a book out of his backpack, a somewhat dubious neo-Heideggerean tract called *How to Save Time* by a minor pragmatic philosopher named Thomas Hawkins. But in his suddenly relaxed frame of mind, he isn't in the mood to read just now, so he places it on the nightstand.

Zord appears there, releasing a petite Martian fart in the direction of the book. "So . . . How's the little quest coming?"

Patrick is a little shocked at first because he hasn't seen Zord since he left Lyonness, but he quickly settles into acceptance of the intrusion. "Well, I thought I had something this morning, but now I don't know. If I can relax for a couple of days, maybe I can get my thoughts back on track."

Zord gestures to the Hawkins book. "Absolute idealism isn't going to help."

"It's not idealism; it's anti-realism. You, of all . . . you should be able to tell the difference."

"That's a matter of perspective, I think. Damn your nonsense-isms anyway. It's all the same neo-anti-everything."

Patrick decides to ignore him and go back to reading his book, but he's distracted by the little guy's beady stare, so he closes the book. "What are you doing here?"

"Just showed up to see how you're doing . . . and to encourage you to go home before you cause any more damage."

"Oh, come on. Is that the best you can come up with? There's nothing for me there anyway."

"Right. You're on a 'quest.' Your quest is bullshit. I told you so in the beginning."

"I assume you mean that in a pragmatic sense."

"Damn your so-called pragmatism. I'm telling you something about the real world here, your real life, and what you call 'pragmatism' has you occupied in this futile adventure, blissfully ignorant of the trail of destruction you leave in your wake."

Zord disappears in a poof. The New Year's Eve photograph he stole from Dorian's house is out on the bedside table. In it he and Ashley both look content, but there's something wrong with both of them, something lost in their eyes. They are there in the same place, but not really together. Their contentment is solitary. To try and clear his mind of thoughts about the past, however recent, he reads another chapter of his book and then settles in for a nap.

Chapter 14

Light is fading outside the square, fiberglass windows of Pell's workshop. Another masterpiece is complete, as he screws in the last hinge on the front door of a two-story Victorian, one of his best sellers. He places the dollhouse on another table, a staged plot of land complete with Astroturf, and snaps a few digital photos from various angles, then moves to the house onto a shelf with its unsold brethren: a beach house, a ranch house, a houseboat, and a scale model of his own Ragnell Oaks, considerably more gussied up than the original, life in miniature being something he feels he has more control over than life in lifesize.

He reckons the Victorian is ready to sell, turns to his laptop, where he navigates to a popular auction website, cuts and pastes text from an old ad for a similar model, makes a few minor modifications, and then posts.

To celebrate, he takes a few nips from a mason jar, his own recipe forged in a copper still in back of the workshop. His own kind of alchemy. Just a couple of sips, though. His stomach is queasy again.

Not quite ready to begin another house, he turns his attention to other miniatures—specifically, a version of himself he's carving out of some leftover wood. A notch here to form the chin, another there to finish off the nose. An uncanny likeness, he thinks, if still naked and colorless. He places the figurine in the houseboat and ships himself off toward faraway lands. In this embodiment of the seafaring stories he read in his youth, he is king of whatever part of the sea he happens to pass over.

From the helm, he surveys his briny green dominion, as far as he can see in any direction, nothing but a gently undulating stillness. That ocean smell soaks into his clothes, the sun warming his face, only a few wispy traces of clouds in the sky. He's after no seabirds or white whales. If any pirates or sea storms should come asking after him, he'll meet them face on, but for now, he only wants to drift in quiet serenity to wherever the wide blue sea may take him, never mind that he may run out of fuel somewhere miles from land. Perhaps his next project should be to build himself a sailboat.

The daydreaming is interrupted by a scratching at the door: Wilhelmina, warning him that it's almost suppertime. He lets the pig inside and tosses her a couple of treats from a copper tin near his work bench. Then he locks up and heads back to the main house, Wilhelmina trotting along at his heels

༃

At 6:30, Patrick wanders downstairs where the rest of the tenants already are assembled. Two men and two women sit at the table. Pell, the fisherman he met earlier, looks rather more peaked than he was in the afternoon.

Clara sets the places then brings out dishes of cornbread, collard greens, slaw, and fried catfish. Very little is said beyond introductions. Linn is a doctor—a general practitioner from Atlanta who's vacationing here to get away from the city for a few days. He looks like the Brawny man—tall, blond and with a walrusy yellow mustache. The two ladies are elderly twin sisters named Penny and Mag. They both have hoarse voices and solid, dark gray hair rolled into a bun, and they both smell like olive oil. Patrick assumes they're long-term residents, as they don't appear to come with any backstory.

The only sounds are the sloppy gnawing of catfish, some muffled compliments to the chef, and an occasional belch. The iced tea is so sweet that it's almost syrupy, but Patrick drinks it down without complaint and even asks for seconds.

After a little while, most everyone is finished eating. During the relative silence, Linn attempts a line of conversation. "So, Patrick. Are you a student?"

Mrs. Ragnell gives him a sharp look, but Patrick gestures that it's okay to ask. "Not officially. I haven't been in school for a couple of years, but I am studying philosophy, sort of informally."

"Really, I was a philosophy major myself in college. Not much good for getting you a job is it?"

"No. But that's not my main priority right now."

"What is?"

"Just, you know, being."

"Well, good luck with that. What philosophers do you like?"

"I've been thinking a lot about Heidegger lately."

"Bah, that's not philosophy. That's just some kind of crazy poetry. Serious philosophers are interested in creating a theoretical backbone for hard science. Existentialism is for kids and people who aren't smart enough to work with logical forms. Besides, he was a Nazi."

Patrick thinks that is an interesting point from a guy who looks like he could be a spokes model for the Aryan Nation. The doctor sounds a lot like Zord, Patrick thinks. He wonders if the little Martian is somehow trying to argue with him through this guy. Then he laughs at himself for that thought, that the demigods would manipulate his reality in such a way . . . then he stops laughing.

After a moment, disguising his discomfort by taking a long swig of iced tea, he pulls himself together to answer Linn's charge. "As I understand it, his acquiescence to the Nazi agenda was just a way to buttress his own power within the German university system. It had no real bearing on his core philosophy."

"There's a little branch of philosophy called Ethics that he might have paid some attention to."

"Everybody makes mistakes."

The ladies at the table are all fidgeting, clearly uncomfortable with the tone of this conversation. Pell mentions something about his father fighting in the second World War, and the twins join him in a brief digression about how the country got behind that war, in contrast to the way people responded to Vietnam and other, more recent international incidents, et cetera. Linn continues without regard to this side discussion.

"I think you're ill-informed about the seriousness of Heidegger's participation with the National Socialist Party. History will reveal all eventually, but anyway, my opinion of such things as phenomenology, existentialism and deconstructionism stands regardless."

Patrick shrugs and turns to Mrs. Ragnell. "Thanks for dinner. It was delicious."

Chapter 15

Root. Snort. Willie is a pig. Of this, if not much else, she is certain. A female pig, a sow. She stands by the pier in the afternoon, rooting near the water's edge. She doesn't wallow. She can go indoors to cool off. If she gets too dirty, the people will rinse her with a hose and dry her off before she goes inside.

She had an operation when she was young, so she could not have piglets even if there were another pig around to provide the seed. Even though she's the only pig in the house, she is not lonely. There are always people in the house, and there are chickens and goats, and sometimes there are squirrels near the woods. Once in a while there is a fish in the water, sometimes dead. When the ladies have tea, one of them might share a cookie with her. She's only allowed in the yard with the goats and chickens in the mornings when the lady goes to get eggs and milk. But sometimes she lingers by the road on the outside of the fence making faces at the hens and their ridiculous gesticulations.

Tired of rooting for now, she roams around the edge of the lake down a path through the woods, to her favorite place, the garden, with its cool stones and shady stalks of corn. The old brick building there has comfortable padded benches. She naps there for a while, dreaming lightly of treats buried in the dirt.

When she's rested and ready for her dinner, she trots up to the small house where the man does his work.

A few days have passed into obscurity at the Ragnell's lakeshore boarding house. Patrick spends his time reading, swimming in the lake, sparring with Linn over philosophy, and roaming freely with his thoughts. Although the actual grounds of Ragnell Oaks seem to be wasting away, there are thick woods nearby that Patrick finds excellent for wandering, honeycombed with clear, inviting footpaths. Unlike the woods around Lyonness, where the trails are narrow and forge through like interlopers, these are wide and sprinkled with pebbles, making them feel more inviting—not as sinister as woods can sometimes be.

The path he's following today comes to an end at a small abandoned chapel. There must have been an actual community around here once. The door of the chapel is broken open, and he goes inside. Moldy air and patches of mud on the half-dozen pews that sit in a single row. But the stained glass windows are intact and cast an orange glow on the otherwise barren room. It feels peaceful. He sits down.

Perhaps, he thinks, the ennui he's been experiencing is somehow spiritual, a deficiency of some kind. Not that he's going to suddenly start believing in God or anything crazy like that. The spirituality he has in mind has something to do with a sense of how he fits in with everything else in the world, how his actions affect others for better or for worse.

Could be he's starting to feel guilty again about leaving Ashley. Maybe Zord was right and he should just go home, try to pick up where they left off like they've done so many times before. But something is definitely different, more serious, about their separation this time around.

He exits the chapel and, around the corner, stumbles on what must be Mrs. Ragnell's dirty little secret. Her garden is in the chapel's graveyard. Spread among the cornstalks, tomato stakes and cabbage heads are a dozen or more headstones. He makes his way through, checking out the grave markers. The most recent one he can find is over fifty years old. After thinking it over a few minutes, he decides to his own surprise that this doesn't particularly creep him out. Although he wonders if later, when he reaches for a piece of cornbread at the dinner table, he'll feel a bit like a cannibal.

Leaving the wood, he comes across the Ragnell's pet pig rooting around at the lake's edge. Willie really digs in there, committed wholeheartedly to whatever she's searching for. Wonder if she knows what it is. Finds himself a little envious.

Chapter 16

Early Friday, Clara is just finishing her morning chores—milk the goat, collect a few eggs, water the vegetable garden. Willie trots along behind her as she flits from one end of the property to another. Finally, with Pell out on the lake and the boarders all still sleeping, it's Clara's favorite time of day, her personal time. After dumping a load of clothes into the washer, she steps onto the back porch with a fresh cup of coffee and Willie at her side, breathing in the morning dew. She sits. She sighs. If only they could afford to fix the place up a little more, offer a few more amenities, she could justify increasing their rates. Of course, she'd let Penny and Mag stay on at the old rate, just because they've been there forever. Maybe she should go into town and try to get a loan.

The sun is just up and immaculate over the lake, shining with a magnificence that seems to her almost royal. There's even a regal purple tint to the sky this morning. She thinks she can see a bubbling up in the lake on the horizon. The disturbance comes and goes, inching closer each time she sees it.

Patrick skips breakfast. With the sky inflamed, threatening to storm—instead of taking a walk, he decides to tarry off on his bike, explore the mountains that overshadow the lake. As the roads wind and ascend, changing from asphalt to red clay, the rainclouds remain demure, letting loose only a smattering of light showers. Whenever he looks to his right, toward the center of the mountain, Patrick thinks he sees the crest approaching, but the road just keeps going up and up. He knows that on the other side of the mountain, there's a little town where Clara sometimes, for special occasions, goes for groceries.

Here the woods clear a bit, and the slope steepens, but the footpath continues. Patrick catches a glimpse of a structure, perhaps a cabin overlooking the valley, and he decides to park his motorcycle and follow the trail on foot to see if it leads there.

It seems to take forever, but he finally reaches the cabin. Perhaps because Heidegger has been on his mind, it reminds him of pictures he's seen of the secluded cabin at Todnauberg, the Black Forest retreat where Martin H. wrote some of his most famous work. There's even a water pump and trough. The cabin itself is basic, small, almost a shack. The front door looks wide open.

Patrick peeks inside and doesn't see anybody. He shouts hello; no answer. He spots some bottles of wine on a rack, which reminds him that he hasn't had a drink since he got here. He carefully puts two of the bottles in his pack, wrapping them in his spare shirts for protection. Twenty feet away is a huge drop off where you can look right into the valley for miles around. He unzips and takes a piss off the side of the mountain, then rushes back down the trail to his bike.

Back at the Ragnells, just in time for dinner, he announces that he picked up some gifts in town, and he presents the two bottles of red wine. Mrs. Ragnell almost loses her deadpan composure for a second, even seems excited. "Oh, that's a lovely gesture Patrick. Thank you."

"No problem."

ॐ

It's nice, Clara thinks, to have some wine with dinner. Nicer still to have some after dinner. Of course, many bed and breakfast establishments have a refined cocktail hour in the evening. Why don't they? She's still learning the business, she supposes, and she knows nothing about wine. This wine Patrick brought is wonderful though. Maybe she should try to learn something about it, subscribe to a magazine or something.

Mag is a teetotaler, but Penny has had three or four glasses and seems a bit tipsy. Suddenly, it occurs to her—she's entertaining guests. She never does this. She just leaves them to their own devices, except at tea time and meals. Eyeing some old vinyl records on a shelf in the corner, she asks if anyone would like to hear some music. When everyone has nodded to general consensus, she pulls out an Ella Fitzgerald LP. The records obviously had belonged to Pell's parents; funny that she'd never thought about them much before. They were just more knickknacks decorating the parlor shelves.

When the piano intro to "That Old Black Magic" comes in, Linn reaches out his hand in an offer to dance. He's very light on his feet, and they glide over the rug. Pell and Patrick move the coffee table to clear some space. Mag and Penny dance together in a lively sort of jitterbug. At the beginning of the next tune, Pell taps Linn on the shoulder and cuts in. She can't remember the last time she danced with her husband.

As the record continues, they all dance—Linn and Patrick taking turns trading off with the twins. When the static of the needle signifies the end of Side A, Penny turns excitedly to her sister. "Mag, you must go and get your ukulele!"

"Oh, no. I couldn't . . ."

Clara didn't even know Mag had a ukulele. She really should get to know these ladies a little better, she thinks. Everyone begs Mag to fetch her instrument, and she finally relents. In a minute, she's back downstairs, ukulele in hand. She strums a dominant seventh chord and then begins singing "By the Light of the Silvery Moon" in a light, tuneful soprano, finishing to enthusiastic applause.

"Play that song you wrote Mag."

After some initial protests, she begins a drawn out shanty.

Oh, you devious beast of the lake!
What a horrible sight you make.
At the dawn and the twilight time, you
Silhouette the horizon line.
Are you demon or plesiosaurus?
Will you e'er show your face before us?

The boatmen exclaim your infamous name—
Tallulah! Tallulah!
You don't mean us no harm, do ya?

Oh you hideous beast of the lake,
You mischievous yellow-eyed snake.
You make all the young girls scream
When you wake them from midnight dreams.

All across Alabam and Georgia,
All hail the monster Tallulah!

The boatmen exclaim your infamous name—
Tallulah! Tallulah!
You don't mean us no harm, do ya?

Clara looks at Mag cross-eyed and claps politely, and gradually the others join her in smattering applause. Mag looks pleased with her performance. Before she can start another number, there's a knock at the window. A welcome interruption as far as Clara is concerned, though Penny nearly jumps out of her seat at the sound. It's Henry Bollinger, who lives in a cabin up the mountain. Clara goes out the back door to see what he wants.

Bollinger is an odd little man. One wouldn't be blamed for comparing him to a troll with his long beard and slumped posture. He says someone broke into his cabin while he was out hunting and wonders if she's seen anybody suspicious.

"I haven't seen anybody suspicious, Henry. But if I do I'll let you know. Was anything taken?"

She can't imagine that he owns anything worth stealing. He says that some booze is missing. She tells him it was probably some rowdy teenagers from town and wishes him a good night. When she returns to the drawing room, everyone seems to be milling around waiting to find out what the commotion was about. Clara says it's nothing, just a neighbor who lost something. She feigns a yawn and declares herself wiped out for the evening. One by one, Pell and the boarders follow suit.

Chapter 17

Saturday afternoon, Patrick wanders down to the small structure Pell uses as a workshop. He wonders what its original purpose was. Perhaps it was the slaves' quarters, if the house is indeed that old. Seems to him like every story he ever hears about this part of the world, no matter what else it might touch on, ends up being about race in one way or another. That or incest. He wonders how his own story fits into that, if his family ever owned any slaves. As far back as he's ever traced, which isn't far—his grandparents all passed when he was young, and he never really knew much about any of them—they've always been working class. They never owned much of anything except a modest house here and there, and it's hard to imagine any great-grandfather of his in the financial position to own any slaves. Easy enough to imagine some version of his father running the whip, but owning . . . that's another question. And if they did, what ever happened to those people after they were emancipated? Are their descendents still walking around Lyonness, working in the kitchen at the Kettle Diner, attending the sidewalk breakfast for the homeless at his mother's church? Remarkable how silent the whole history is, or maybe he just wasn't curious enough.

Patrick shakes off this thought and notices for the first time that there's a copper still in back of the building, smells ripe. He hasn't seen one of these since he was a kid. A friend of his father's had one, but he didn't use it anymore since the county went wet. Guess that's at least partly what keeps old Pell busy out here.

Around the corner, he peeks into the doorway. Pell is sitting at a bench, diligently at work on something Patrick can't see. He must have heard the footsteps because he turns around suddenly, dropping a small wooden figurine he was carving.

"Sorry, I didn't mean to . . . guess I was just being nosy. Didn't know anybody was in here."

"Ain't hiding anything."

"Whatcha working on back here?"

"Odds 'n ends."

"So . . . you gonna let me sample some of that white lightning you're cooking back there?"

The old man grins wide. "Sure. Come on in. Most people think that still back there is just an antique, which it is, but it's never been out of use."

Patrick steps into the small room, looking around while Pell scuttles around, presumably searching for a glass. The pig follows him in, sniffing around on the floor. In the back, there are neat stacks of various kinds of wood, some cardboard boxes, plastic bins, a table saw and other power tools. It smells like paint and sawdust. He's not sure how Pell can hang out in here. Guess the moonshine probably helps. Another wall is nearly full, ceiling to floor with shelves holding gorgeous houses—toys, he guesses.

"These are amazing. Such detail. You made these I presume."

"I ain't just whittling dicks in here."

Pell pours a yellow-brown liquid from a jug into a mason jar and hands it to Patrick. The odor is pungent, yet sweet. The old man pours a small amount into a dish on the floor, and the pig slurps at it.

"It's okay for him to drink that?"

"Her. She loves it, but I only give her a taste. It's an old family recipe, goin' back at least four generations. Mostly corn. We got a lot of that around here."

"Not bad. Certainly has a kick to it . . . Hey, I think your pig just ate whatever you just dropped on the floor when I came in."

"Shit . . . Willie, did you eat that?"

The pig gives him a wide-eyed, innocent look as Pell bends down and pries its mouth open.

"Guess you swallered it already . . . Dammit, Willie, I been working on that for two days."

All of a sudden, Pell doubles over with a groan, and Patrick rushes over to him, picks him up. The bulky fisherman leans heavily on Patrick's shoulder, and he has to almost drag him the first few steps. After that Pell puts some of his weight back on his own feet and can walk with minimal assistance. At the short set of steps to the back door, Patrick gives him a boost from the armpits and they clamber into the kitchen.

Slowly, they make their way through the dining area to the parlor sofa. Patrick is nervous. He's not sure what questions to ask to start figuring out what's wrong and what to do. But somehow, he calms himself enough to attempt some reassurance. "It's gonna be okay, old man. There's a doctor in the house."

"It's my stomach. Had the runs for a few days now."

Armed with this information, Patrick lays the old man down, then runs upstairs, knocking on a couple of doors until he finds Linn's. "Pell is real sick. Can you look at him? He's in the parlor."

Linn, still in a bathrobe, grabs a black bag and follows Patrick downstairs. Clara is there already, patting down his head with a wet towel.

Patrick leaves the doctor to his work, goes back to his room and stares at the walls for a few minutes. He decides to go to the bathroom before confining himself to his quarters for the rest of the night, but the lavatory nearest to his room is occupied. When he knocks, he hears Penny's gruff voice. "It'll be a while, looks like."

He stands at the top of the stairs looking down on the patriarch of the house, who seems to be having a hallucinatory fit, his eyes rolled back in his head and his face slack with terror. Pell mumbles a few incoherent phrases and claws at the air as if fending off some invisible attacker. Patrick is stricken with fear himself, frozen by indecision. What can he do?

Fortunately, Linn restrains the old man. After a minute or two, Pell settles down and even seems to fall asleep, and his face is as serene and sage as the Buddha. Clara and Linn look on like wise men in a crèche. Then, suddenly, the old man wakes up screaming, his eyes glowing neon blueLinn gives him a shot of something that calms him again, and he goes back to sleep.

Later, Linn joins Patrick in his room, and they share a drink, some single-malt Scotch that Linn brought with him. He tells Patrick that Pell has a vitamin deficiency called pellagra.

"Pretty rare these days since they started fortifying most store-bought breads and such with all the vitamins you need. But because they grow or catch a lot of their own food here . . ."

"Their diet is lacking in . . . whatever vitamin."

"Niacin."

"Right. Interesting."

"It's nothing for you to worry about, unless you plan to stay here indefinitely. Even then, if they take my advice, the diet around here will change. I've already spoken to Clara about it." He chuckles.

"I have to admit, though, this episode has given my vacation a bit more of the 'old South' feeling than I actually bargained for. Anyway, my vacation ends tomorrow. Good thing I was still here when this happened."

Patrick agrees that it's lucky, says goodnight to Linn and everyone else, and he locks himself in his room. He's glad he could be a little bit useful tonight. He's started to feel like he's actually fitting in here, a strange sensation for him.

The picture of him and Ashley with Dorian and Karen is still on the bedside table, as is the copy of *Cacophony* that he took from their launch party. He puts all that stuff in a drawer by the bed. Perhaps he could stay on here indefinitely if he can find a way to generate some income, maybe do some kitchen work in town or even bottle and sell some of Pell's moonshine. He can't really think about it; he is thoroughly exhausted and doesn't even read the next chapter of his book before he goes to sleep.

Chapter 18

Nearly a week has gone by, and Pell is recovering fine. As she vacuums the hallway upstairs, Clara thinks that it hasn't been so bad going into town every few days for some groceries, although it is starting to stretch their budget. They have savings, but it isn't much, and she'd rather not touch it. Pell sold a couple of dollhouses recently, which has helped, and Patrick has been lending a hand around the house, freeing up some of her time for shopping. Speaking of Patrick, he went off again in the morning, and she hasn't heard from him. She doesn't know if he'll be back for supper.

Linn very kindly recommended the place to a colleague who will be coming to stay with them in a few days. She's decided to raise the rates a little, which she hates to do, but she knows it won't make any difference to the doctor.

Clara unplugs the vacuum just in time to hear the phone. It's the sheriff's office.

"Yes, I know a Patrick Alexander. He's been staying at our place . . . Okay, I'll be there as soon as I can."

She hangs up the phone and calls out to Pell, soon realizing that he's probably in his workshop and can't hear her. So she high tails it down the stairs and out back, doesn't bother to knock before bursting in, and she's startled by his being startled. Then she finally catches her breath.

"Get your keys. Patrick's been arrested."

"What's that got to do with me?"

"C'mon, Pell."

As they drive into town, she explains that Patrick got caught breaking into Henry's cabin up on the hill. It was probably all just a misunderstanding of some kind, but they'll straighten it all out.

Patrick can see them come in from where he sits, a familiar look of disappointment splashed across both of their faces. The hallway seems a mile long, and it seems to take forever for Clara and Pell to get to his cell. It occurs to him that they design these places to maximize the guilt you feel when your friend, lawyer or parent comes to get you out. He's still not sure why he did it. He figures he had such a good time the last Friday that he wanted to repeat the ritual, but this time, the old geezer walked in on him, armed with a rifle.

When Pell and Clara finally get there, they just look at him through the bars, shaking their heads. It takes a minute before Clara finally says something.

"Well, it comes down to this. I've spoken to Henry, and to the sheriff, and they've agreed to drop the charges down to a misdemeanor if you get out of town tonight. You'll just have to pay a fine, and you won't have to go to court."

He nods his head. He suspected he'd screw this up somehow. Could have been worse, he supposes.

"Patrick, we like you. We really do. But we do think it's best that you take advantage of the sheriff's offer."

The fine uses up almost all the money he has left anyway. He guesses he'll have to go back to Birmingham, try and get a job, figure things out from there. When they arrive at the house, he quietly packs his bag and departs without fanfare.

Chapter 19

Demigods disburse into waves and particles, a pulse over a copper wire that stretches from Lyonness to a local exchange station near Columbus, Mississippi; a series of ones and zeroes traveling over a fiber optic cable to a main exchange station in Tupelo then to another in Gainesville, Florida; a signal routed to a cell phone tower at the corner of University Avenue and Main Street. Patrick's phone rings, but he doesn't hear it. The speaker emitting the ring is tight against his leg inside the pocket of his blue jeans, and the music in Full Circle is loud, even though the nightclub isn't yet open.

He likes the fact that the place is called Full Circle; he's had a thing about circles lately. But he doesn't like the logo, which is circular, but it's more of a spiral design and not especially suggestive of a "full" circle. There's been an eerie peace ever since Patrick got to Florida. It's the middle of August, and perhaps the heat has either cleared such distractions from his mind or slowed them to a halt.

He's finished setting out the rows of metal chairs onto the open dance floor in front of the stage, and he awaits further instructions from Victoria. She's nervous and afraid nobody's going to show up. She keeps straightening her bright green swooped wig, although it isn't ever at all crooked. Just below the hem of her short green, checkered dress, her yellow, garterless stockings are defying gravity, looking as if they could, at any moment, slip down to her ankles, and yet they hold fast, even as she paces quickly from one corner of the room to the other. Presumably to cover the fact that she is not really doing anything useful and merely pacing, she occasionally asks questions of Rich the bartender who answers with a series of friendly grunts and shrugs.

There's nothing for Patrick to do either. He's simply early. Rich hasn't opened the bar yet, but he passes Patrick a pint of Guinness on the house. To pass the time, he retrieves a book from his backpack, the aptly titled *Being on Time,* by Thomas Hawkins, a follow up to his earlier work *How to Save Time*. While he thumbs through it to find his place, Victoria is testing the microphone. Rich interrupts, trying to make polite convo.

"So . . . How'd you and Vic meet?"

"Long story."

And it is.

After he left the Ragnells', he spent a couple of days driving around the countryside, camping out in the woods. Nothing much happened, except a few inconsequential demigod encounters (a fact he doesn't share with Rich, for obvious reasons). Then he finally decided that he'd return to Birmingham after all. It took him about an hour and a half to get to Dorian's house. Nobody was home, so he began writing a note, but someone walked up behind him—Rebecca, arms full of groceries. He put the unwritten note in his pocket. When he'd asked what she was doing there, she'd stared at him coldly. After a moment she said that she had moved in with Dorian and Karen and that they'd actually become quite close. She emphasized the word close. A lot had happened in the past few weeks apparently.

As she unpacked boxes of organic breakfast cereal from her hemp net grocery bags, Rebecca mentioned casually that Ashley had been there. "I was surprised when I saw her. I didn't think she was your type."

He's pretty sure the implication is that Ashley looks like "white trash," and he challenges Rebecca on this, she says never mind and changes the subject.

"Anyway, she said if we saw you to tell you to call her, so I'm telling you to call her."

Seconds later, he'd already forgotten the message, although he did eventually call Ashley, a month or so later, gave her his address in Florida so she could mail him the divorce papers. But he's digressing . . .

He recalls admiring Rebecca as she fluttered around the kitchen, opening and closing cabinets, like a hummingbird. Her silence was a deliberate silence. Her being was a deliberate being. But then he saw that her eyes were beginning to swell with tears, and his head was suddenly filled with brain noise, and he could hardly hear her talking, just like when he used to argue with Ashley, just like in all the moments he's least proud of.

"Look, I'm sorry that I took off like that, especially right after . . . what we did, but, you know, what about me, my needs?"

"You look. Just get the fuck out of my house. I don't ever want to see you again."

Get the fuck out is just what he did. It was still early in the afternoon, so he'd cruised through Five Points to see if anything interesting was happening. A couple of faux-hawked teenagers were hanging out by the fountain, but not much else. As he wound through the greenery of Highland Avenue, he saw a familiar face loading a moving truck. It was Victoria, Rebecca's co-editor from the magazine, somehow looking glamorous in a tee shirt and torn shorts, looking relaxed even while dragging furniture into the back of a large truck. He offered to give her a hand.

"That would be awesome actually. I called about ten of my friends to come help me move, and no one showed up. I've been saving the heavy stuff for last."

Patrick helped her carry a chest of drawers, a sofa, a couple of bookshelves, and a wooden bed frame into the truck. When everything was in the truck and tied down, she still had room to spare.

"Jesus, I should have gotten a smaller truck. Want to move anything to Florida?"

"Do you have room in the back for my motorcycle?"

"You serious?"

That was both what Vic said then and what Rich is saying now. Rich refills Patrick's pint glass while commenting further. "A spontaneous romantic adventure. Hell of a place to end up though. How long ago was that?"

"About eight weeks I guess. Maybe a little longer."

During that time, through a network of earnest young vegans, he found employment in a record store whose specialty is music distributed in unconventional packaging—manila envelopes, cereal boxes, shoe boxes, candy wrappers, as well as otherwise normal record, cassette and CD casings in non-traditional sizes and shapes. They share space with a used book dealer and a video rental shop that carries only old B movies and kitsch.

He's also sold his bike and bought a converted van, 1984 Ford Econoline, blue and silver with a blue and gray interior. Except the passenger side captain's chair is red because he accidentally spilled battery acid on the original.

"Is it love?" Rich wants to know.

"I don't know. Maybe."

They'd loaded the motorcycle into the back of the moving truck, and then passed the first hour in virtual silence, although the radio was on, tuned to a classic rock station, playing songs that one or the other of them sheepishly admitted to always having liked. It broke the ice a bit. When they reached Montgomery a little more than an hour later, it began to rain. At a stop light on South Boulevard in front of the mall, she confided in him. "I have to be honest with you. I didn't like you when I met you at that party. And the things Rebecca told me about you weren't terribly flattering either."

"Then why did you agree to let me come along?"

"I don't know. Let's just say I like to make my own judgments about people. I don't know you, or rather I only really know you through other people's eyes. And, frankly, you seem sort of dangerous, and that's appealing to me."

"Well, that's sound reasoning in my book."

"What is the town like where you come from?"

"Lyonness? I like to say that it's a little town that's much bigger than it seems."

"Oh."

He was going to ask where she grew up, but he knows. He saw her picture on the mantel at Ragnell Oaks, and he also saw her surname—Ragnell, natch—on the moving van paperwork that lay between them on the bench seat. Before he could follow up with more questions about that, her undergraduate work, what brought her to Birmingham, and any other mundane personal facts he may have been able to glean from her, she announced that she had to pee and pulled into a rest stop.

After the stop, he took over the driving for a little while, and

Victoria fell asleep, her cherubic face silent and still, framed by her boyish blonde hair. A leap of faith, he thought, just closing your eyes and letting this stranger deliver you to your destination, something he wasn't sure he could do, although he was doing just that in a way. But his eyes were open.

Just as he had heard the hum of his motorcycle as a kind of mantra, he now heard the eternal *om* of the truck's engine, now even more intensely ever before. Larger engine than the bike, to be sure, but also it's not as personal, not purring right between your legs. Monkeyman appeared perched silently on the dashboard, with his feet resting on the knobs of the stereo. But he remained there only a moment, with a serene smile, as if to say, you're going the right direction.

After supper at some fast food restaurant on the interstate, she drove. Sooner than they expected, they arrived at her new apartment in Gainesville, and he stayed the night—ultimately stayed on indefinitely. They'd shared a bottle of Scotch to celebrate the move, and, with little fanfare, they ended up sleeping together. The sex was intense, acrobatic. They fucked in every room in the house, and they both slept soundly afterwards. Just thinking about it now, he still gets aroused.

Although they had a strange, distant relationship for the first couple of weeks, he and Victoria have generally gotten along like the best of friends the past couple of months, like a regular couple in fact. Something about her . . . almost makes him forget himself.

Back in the present, the DJ has shown up, and Victoria is asking him where the Kale Dancers are. The DJ is the boyfriend of one of the dancers.

"Dude, we've spent the last thirty hours really getting in touch with kale. I mean really. Thirty hours. So, in light of that, I just want to let you know that they've changed the dance some. But you've got nothing to worry about. They'll be here."

Through a series of position changes and inadvertent collisions, the phone in Patrick's pocket has managed to turn itself off. Otherwise, he almost certainly would have heard it ring this time, since the volume of the music overhead has died down significantly. Also, he happens to think to look at the phone right at the moment that the call was being transmitted, in case he had missed any calls. In the time it takes for him to turn the phone back on and for the phone to register a signal, the call has already been transferred to his voice mail, which he has never learned how to check.

He wanders outside. It is a muggy August evening in Gainesville, and Main Street is lifeless. Patrick considers going to the bar across the street to kill some time, see if anyone he knows is around, but before he gets a chance to cross the road, a shirtless gutter punk on a bicycle asks him if he knows what's going on here tonight.

"Yeah. It's a show called 'Consciousness and Cabbage.' There's some performance art, spoken word, music and stuff like that. The cover is $5, and the money is going to the help the volunteers who are cleaning up water lettuce in the Itchetucknee. It starts at 8."

Thanking him for the information, the kid remounts his Schwinn and disappears around the corner.

This time when his phone rings, he hears it and answers.

Demigods stir, but remain silent, out of sight, hidden in pillars of cigarette smoke, rising into the ether. A sharp, high-pitched squeal emanates from the speakers and then is quickly squelched by the downward motion of a slider on the soundboard. Gradually, the sound of sound—that low, warm hum with the potential of sound—begins to form out of the nothingness. And then a few simple words—check, checking, one, two, one, two . . .

Once Victoria is satisfied with the volume and quality of the p.a. system, she heads for the bathroom. She wipes off the seat, hikes up her dress, and then sits, ruminating about the void of the empty stage. Trying not to think about the fact that the Kale Dancers haven't shown up yet, that that's the one part of the show they never got to rehearse, that the DJ is tripping or something, that there are lines she meant to memorize but didn't, that the lighting in here will make it impossible to read from her script, and that the stage is actually much smaller than she originally thought.

First the void, then the word. That's how things begin, and as she swirls these words around her mouth, extracting nuances of flavor from them, she realizes that there is little she finds more agitating than an empty stage—agitating like someone shaking your shoulders and insisting that you get out of bed, shower, get dressed and do something.

When she returns to the bar, she is relieved to see that a number of people have arrived. Somebody is even at the door collecting the cover charge, and the two dancers, blithe and slender in their green tights and kale skirts, fritter about near the entry way. She orders a Tom Collins and wonders where Patrick has gotten off to. She scans the room for the spiked tips of his hair, which tend to stand above the crowds. The DJ has set up his turntables and has started playing "Pass the Dutchie." God, she didn't know he was going to be so cheesy. This girl, Suzie, comes in wearing a paper tiara and carrying a cardboard sign that reads, "Will dance for money," and the Kale Dancers are trying to convince her to join them. Suzie already has the tights for it. The dancers, along with Suzie—adorably arty with her frizzed out blonde hair and horn rimmed glasses—approach Victoria purposefully, repeating what the DJ told her earlier re: the last 30 hours and the really getting in touch with kale.

Victoria sips her drink through the thin stirring straw, expressionless.

"That's great; it's your piece. Just do me a favor and go over the changes with Don, the accordion player. He's the guy in the cow-print lingerie standing by the DJ booth. Just make sure it works with his music."

It's getting close to 8:00 and the club closes at 11:00 because it's Sunday, so she begins to feel like she needs to get the show started. She navigates her way toward the stage between the bodies crowding the bar and the rows of metal chairs, borrowed from the Civic Media Center and transported here in the back of Jimmy Nil's pickup truck. Once atop the small platform at the front of the room, she taps the microphone.

"Excuse me, everybody! Hi. Welcome to tonight's cabaret, Consciousness and Cabbage. This is the third cabaret show that I've organized this year, and they have all been benefits for the CMC. Many of you know . . ."

About halfway through the delivery of her opening spiel, it begins to deliver itself, the agitating void slowly dilating, and giving birth to drama. She flips the bobbed ends of her blue wig and opens her heart to the standing room only crowd.

She is the beginning of the universe, the big bang. She makes art happen.

After introducing the first act, she lightly steps off the stage and drifts back to the bar to watch. Patrick is there, interrupting her stellar moment with a despairing look. He whispers hoarsely.

"Sorry I disappeared. My mother called. My father came back."

Patrick has a way of setting up these moments of suspense when he speaks, like the universe will suddenly freeze, a sharp violin will ring out a minor chord, and then they will cut to a commercial. After these weeks with him, she's learning when to refrain from ending that moment too soon, so she reflects his grave gaze back at him. She recalls his story of the disappearing patriarch, the primary purpose of which has usually been anecdotal explanation for certain quirks of his personality. This news, however, seems to require perhaps some action on his part, and he has yet to announce, perhaps yet to decide, what that is to be.

He moves his mouth to speak, but the words seem to come out with difficulty. "Apparently . . ." He leans in closer to her, and she can almost hear the wiry strands of her wig scratching at his lips. "Apparently, he showed up at the church. At a charity breakfast for homeless people. Let's just watch the show. I'll fill in the details for you later."

On stage, their friend Frog, who performs under the name the Amazing Mr. Slug, has just finished setting the stage for what appears to be a life-sized puppet show. Frog wears a robe and a large white mask that resembles a mollusk shell of some kind. His face is hidden, but you can see the bushy ends of his caveman beard curling around the edges. His female assistant, whose identity is unknown to both Patrick and Victoria, is similarly masked.

As Frog takes the stage and his bleeping and blurping sounds fill the large room, Patrick and Victoria sip at their drinks, giving each other occasional sympathetic glances.

Chapter 20

Their one bedroom apartment in Gainesville is on the second floor of a white, 100 year-old, cracker-style house that's been divided into rental units. From the outside, it looks like it might be falling apart; the white paint peels away in most places, and the railings are badly damaged from a past termite infestation (supposedly treated just before Patrick and Vic moved in). But the interiors are recently renovated with glossy hardwood floors, fresh paint and new appliances.

Patrick is in the bathroom where there's a convergence of demigods—with the door open, of course. They're all crowding around him while he's trying to shave, and they're unusually invasive this morning, jostling him for space in the small room. Zord stands on the sink, blocking his view of the mirror, lecturing him about personal responsibility. Monkeyman is on his shoulders whispering a reassuring mantra into his ear. Harold just sits on top of the toilet tank, as usual, occasionally poking Patrick in the gut, making him conscious of his hunger.

"Who are you talking to?"

Victoria's voice from the bedroom. He hadn't realized she was so near. The television was on in the living room, and he assumed she was watching it. "Nobody, babe. Just talking to myself."

Suddenly, she's at the door, and the demigods vanish, maybe behind the shower curtain. "Can I ask you something?"

"Sure."

"Did you buy some kind of chemical drain cleaner?"

He did. She had mentioned the day before that she was going to get some vinegar and baking soda to clean the drains, that she didn't trust those chemicals, but he went behind her back. Ashley always used those hippie homeopathic things, and they never worked. He'd thoughtlessly put the empty bottles in the recycling bin. He guesses, correctly, that she saw them, and he fesses up.

"What's going on with you? You seem weird lately . . . secretive."

"It's nothing."

"I don't know. That's such a weird thing to lie about. I'm not angry. I'm just confused."

It's true, he knows. He is secretive, and he doesn't know why. He hasn't even told her about the time he spent at her parents' place. He knows that she's told them about him. She talks to them on the phone all the time, but they haven't made the connection. He's figured out through her family anecdotes that her parents didn't take over Ragnell Oaks from her grandparents until Victoria left for college. So she never really lived there, which explains a little about how she turned out so healthy and relatively normal.

"I'm going out for some smokes."

"Okay. Whatever . . . I'm going to class in a few minutes, so I'll see you later."

୨୧

Zord floats along beside him as he stamps down the sidewalk, while Monkeyman and Harold trail closely behind. Zord taps him on the shoulder annoyingly while he talks.

"Why not just tell her? It's not a big deal."

"At this point, I'd look completely insane."

"Why are you always running away from things?"

"I'm not running away this time. I just need some air. And some cigarettes."

"I'd like to point something out to you."

"Go ahead."

"Your world is so very small. You're on this 'quest,' but you've barely been anywhere.

A young couple passes by walking a dog, and Patrick catches himself before responding to Zord in front of them. Then it occurs to him that these days, people walk down the street talking to themselves all the time, and he considers just holding the cell phone next to his ear, but he can't bring himself to be that phony, and he's still self-conscious. He stops and watches the couple until they pass the corner, and then speaks only in a harsh whisper."

"What do you mean?"

"You've been in three states, all of which are connected to each other. What about L.A., San Francisco, Chicago, New York, Mexico City, Santiago, Montreal, London, Dublin, Paris, Munich, Berlin, Prague, New Delhi, Shanghai, Tokyo, Jerusalem, Cairo, Johannesburg, Lesotho? You've never been any of these places, not even close. You could be anywhere in the world this time tomorrow."

"Oh, come on. There's still plenty of time in my life to travel. Anyway, Vic and I are moving to New York after she graduates."

At the convenience store, Patrick browses the aisles of cheap snack foods and minor auto parts, looking at everything carefully, but nothing jumps out at him. He grabs a six-pack of beer and then asks the cashier for a box of Camel filterless. He's been smoking filterless lately because filtering things just somehow seems wrong to him.

After making his purchases, he walks the two blocks back to his house in silence. Sitting on the porch, he lights a smoke and then pries the top of a beer bottle with his cigarette lighter. From the porch steps, he can see the bell tower of a nearby church; it begins chiming the beginning of the noon hour, a knell to the death of morning.

"I've been thinking about God."

Zord looks at him incredulously from atop the railing. "Meaning what?"

"Meaning, I don't know exactly. Obviously, not a big white bearded face in the sky."

"The concept of God—any concept, any word—is only meaningful if it refers to something. What does it refer to?"

"Can't it just be a variable? A placeholder for whatever turns out to be meaningful about the human experience, because otherwise, it's difficult to talk about that with other people."

Zord, apparently bemused by the sudden turn in their exchange, seems to think this point over for a few moments before responding. "So what you're telling me is that you say 'God' and mean x, and I say 'God' and mean y, or maybe you mean something different every time you say it, until it's a snowball of conflation. How does that enhance the Great Conversation exactly?"

"OK . . . The things beyond my immediate choices, beyond my own control. Something like that? I mean, at any given moment, I have a whole range of choices I can make—eat a sandwich, go for a walk, rob a bank, take a nap . . . And then there's everything else, everything outside my little circle of immediate influence, and maybe we call that God."

"So it's just another word for chaos. Or circumstance. I still fail to see how that's helpful."

Monkeyman, who has been listening in on this conversation

while swinging from the rafters, abruptly drops to the ground and interrupts. "You know enough to realize that you aren't running the show. But you still think you can somehow create God in your own image, and you put some sort of mask on it so you perhaps don't recognize it as yourself. But in the end, it's just a finger puppet version of yourself, still trying to control everything in the universe."

Patrick thinks about this a minute, then continues to Zord. "Ok, how's this then? I picture God as a circle, or maybe a series of circles within circles. Everything around the perimeter of everyday life."

Zord looks doubtful. "Keep working on that. But I don't know why you want to call it God. "

By now, Patrick has finished his cigarette and the beer, and he goes inside. Victoria has already left. The apartment seems empty without her, even with the demigods following him around like hungry cats.

Suddenly, he realizes that it's almost 12:30, and he has to go to work. He tries to put what's left of the six-pack in his backpack so he can take it with him, but there's not enough room, so he clears some things out and puts the stack of papers and books on top of his dresser.

He zips up his bag, slings it over his shoulder like freshly killed game, and exits.

Chapter 21

Victoria soaks in the bath tub, going over the script of a play she's auditioning for. She would be playing the whore Magdalena, who of course, has a heart of gold. It's kind of an arty, postmodern thing, and not that original of a concept, but it's written by a fellow graduate student, and she likes the dialog.

It's hard to concentrate. She's concerned about Patrick acting so weird. When he's home, which is becoming a rare occurrence, he's so spaced out and distant, it's like he's not even there. And he's always sort of mumbling to himself, and when she asks him what he said, he won't repeat it. He didn't come home after work again tonight. The record store closes at 9:00, and it's now past midnight. She knows that he's in one of the bars nearby—there are four or five where he's a regular—but she doesn't feel like going looking for him. He'll linger there until they close at 2, and then he'll stumble home reeking of whiskey and smoke. It'll still be oozing out of his pores even after he showers. He'll be horny, but he'll be too numb from alcohol to have an orgasm.

His aloofness, she supposes, is one of the things she found attractive about him. But now, she has to wonder sometimes if he has any feelings at all, about anything. God, she's such a girl, she thinks. But, you know, he's in the middle of a divorce, and his father has suddenly shown up out of nowhere after being MIA for twenty years. It really is peculiar that he doesn't seem to have any feelings about that stuff.

She puts her script aside and gets out of the bath. Bubbles slide off her breasts, slip silently back into the soapy water. She sometimes wishes they would cling to her body in strategic locations, like they do in the movies. Not that she has issues with her body, but she just likes to see her life in that sort of romantic light.

She notices on Patrick's dresser a pile of stuff he must have cleaned out of his backpack this morning, including a copy of *Cacophony*, that last one she worked on. It's nice, she thinks, that he held onto it. When she picks it up to flip through it, a photograph falls on the ground. That blonde must be his ex-wife, Ashley. She and Ashley look a lot alike in some ways—the blonde hair, although Victoria's is straight; that flowery sundress Ashley is wearing is something she herself would wear. Is that bad? Would it be worse, she wonders, if they looked too different?

For the next couple of hours, she pads around the apartment, turns on the television, turns it off, updates her blog, typing all her recent thoughts about Patrick (to whom she refers in the blog simply as 'P') and his distant emotions. Maybe it has to do with the news he got about his father recently, but it's getting hard for her to take. She deletes the post because it's getting too personal. What is it, she wonders, that makes some of us want to take our innermost thoughts and put them, not just in writing, but out to the universe for anyone to find?

She thinks that maybe she should get a cat, and then she wonders what Patrick would think about that. He's still not home. Who cares what he thinks? She'll get a fucking cat if she wants to.

She curls up with a pillow between her knees and drifts off to sleep.

The sound of a tussle in the street outside wakes her up—a couple of hookers arguing over turf. Judging from the voices, at least one of them is a transvestite, which is par for the course around here. This happens maybe a couple of times a week. More than once, she's found a transvestite hooker utilizing the swing on the house's front porch to entertain a client. Eventually, after complaints from all the tenants in the house, the landlord took the swing down, as it was attracting too much undesirable attention.

She turns on the light, thinking about calling the cops. It's after 4 am, and Patrick still isn't home. What the fuck? Before she picks up the phone, the police show up anyway—kind enough not to run their siren at this time of night, but the blue and red lights strobe through the window and cascade over the empty white wall at the back of the room. They really should get some art or something, she thinks.

The cops are taking a long time to break up the fight, and Victoria puts on a robe so she can go outside, get a better look at whatever's going on out there. When she steps onto the porch, though, she sees that one of the people arguing with the cops is Patrick—apparently, from what she can make out over the shouting, defending the prostitutes' right of assembly. Soon, the hookers, three of them, are in handcuffs and being escorted to the car. Patrick turns away from the officers with a final contempt-powered wave of his arm. As he approaches the porch, stumbling and slurring, he bluntly says hello to Victoria, as if nothing bizarre had just happened. He kisses her on the cheek and brushes past.

She stands there for a minute, watching as the police drive off and then just staring into the empty space where they had just been. When she goes inside, she finds him passed out on the sofa.

Chapter 22

The Lost Expletives are in town, playing at a club up the street from their house. Patrick walks over to meet up with Josh after the sound check. The first thing Patrick notices is that, in the last six months Josh's hair has gotten really long and falls in big, bouncy curls over his shoulders. It reminds him of how much the world outside his own solipsistic mind can change in a relatively short amount of time. Josh is wearing glasses too, small round ones with a thin wire frame, which he doesn't ever wear on stage, and he looks like someone from a different era altogether.

"Is that a new van outside?" Patrick saw the van on his way in, a brown and white Dodge, an extended 15-seater like the ones used by church choirs. Josh says yes, that he bought it recently at an auto auction, and he had a buddy install a cage in the back for their equipment. They sit at the bar comparing notes about vans for a few minutes, and Josh orders a couple of beers for them.

"So enough about auto-mechanics," Josh says. "How are you doing?"

"Fine. My divorce is almost settled. I work in a record store. I'm living with a woman named Victoria who's going to grad school here, and I really like her. She'll be here later, so you'll meet her then. I'm doing okay. Oh, and apparently the father returned from exile."

"No way."

"Yeah, I haven't seen him, and according to my mother, nobody knows where he's living. He just showed up in town one day."

As they chat, people start to filter into the club. The first are the barflies, older guys who for some reason just hang out here; they claim their perches for the night where they'll sit drinking whatever's cheap. Next is a throng of teenagers, with their punk rock hair primped in all manner of shapes and colors. It's an all-ages show, and the opening act is a local hardcore favorite. When they start playing, the kids all crowd around the stage, moshing and screaming along with the lyrics. Patrick's friends Frog and Suzie show up, and he greets them each with a casual salute. By now, some of the post-grad hipsters and audiophiles have arrived, including a couple of Patrick's employees from the record store.

Victoria also comes in with this group, and Patrick almost doesn't recognize her because she's dyed her hair jet black. Although it takes him by surprise, he thinks it suits her, and in fact, he can't keep his hands off her long enough to introduce her to Josh. She's wearing a black pleather miniskirt and a pink short-sleeved button-down top, sheer stockings and red boots.

"Look at you. You look fantastic!"

While Patrick is busy fondling her, she introduces herself to Josh and shakes hands, raising her voice a bit so it can be heard.

"Patrick's really been talking up this show. He says you guys are the greatest band ever . . . Jeez, Patrick. Save some for later. We're in public here."

"There's an outdoor patio where people go to smoke, and Patrick leads them out so they can talk without the music drowning them out. They make small talk, and Patrick's mind starts to wander a little bit."

From their vantage on the patio, Patrick can see people going into the front door of the club. Oddly, he thinks he sees a girl from his hometown, Cherry Hinderson, looking much the same as she did when he left Lyonness a few months ago, though it makes no sense to him that she would be here, in Florida. He excuses himself and goes inside, but he doesn't see her. Perhaps it wasn't her, or maybe she's just blending in with the crowd.

When he returns to the patio, Josh is in the middle of telling Victoria an anecdote about his and Patrick's brief and fruitless flirtation with break dancing in junior high.

"Patrick was better at it than most of us. I remember one time, at recess, seeing a bunch of black kids crowded together in a circle in the corner of the schoolyard, and they were all clapping their hands and hollering. I went over to see what was going on, and there was Patrick busting a move in the middle of the circle."

Victoria laughs. "I never would have guessed it."

"'Course, shortly some older kids came over and threatened to kick his ass for hangin' out with the 'niggers.'"

"That's awful . . ."

Feeling a bit of tension at the story's let-down ending, Patrick breaks the ice by doing a little robot dance as he walks back up to them.

When the Lost Expletives finally go on, Patrick and Victoria watch from the side of the stage, close enough to see everything but avoid the ruckus of the mosh pit. They're in rare form, and Josh is all over the stage while Louie plays brain-splitting rhythms. James and Fish are jumping around almost as much as Josh, smashing into each other as they play, falling and writhing then getting up to do it all again.

After three songs, Patrick can't sit still anymore. He kisses Victoria on the neck and says he'll be right back, then he leaps right into the middle of the pit, dancing his ass off and flinging the teenage moshers away from him like they're mere pests. After that song ends, he looks back at Victoria, and she's laughing hysterically. He pogos through the next number, jumping onto Frog's shoulders and nearly knocking him over.

When that song is done, he rejoins Victoria. The pit has spread and some of the more aggressive dancers are coming dangerously close to smashing into the both of them. He stands in front of Victoria and fends them off one by one. After a few more songs, he takes her by the hand and drags her to the bathroom, quickly locking the door behind them. He lifts her up onto the sink and pulls off her panties, and they fuck until the set ends.

Sunday morning, Victoria tiptoes between the bodies strewn about her living room so she can make some coffee. The concert was fun, but she wishes Patrick had said something to her before inviting the band to sleep over. Although she wouldn't have objected, these acts of common courtesy just seem to elude him sometimes.

The smell of coffee brewing seems to stir the troops. Josh offers to make breakfast.

"I don't know if we have anything to make," she says.

"No problem. I'll just run down to the store and get some stuff. What do you like? Bagels, eggs, bacon, orange juice?"

She says that any of that sounds great and gives him directions to the store on the corner. He refuses to take any money from her, and she thanks him. While he's gone, she gets coffee cups down from the cabinet, sets out milk, sugar and spoons. Fish wakes up and says he's impressed with how civilized she is.

"The last place we crashed was filthy. You couldn't sit down on the furniture without getting covered in fleas, and there was dog shit on the floor that had been there so long it was petrified. The guy offered to make us some coffee, but we were all scared to use the cups. She laughs and Louie chimes in from his sleeping bag with another story.

"At one place, the roommates entertained themselves playing 'lice roulette.' They put different hats on the floor, and some of them had head lice in them. I don't know how that worked exactly. Seems like all the hats would have lice eventually."

James nods in agreement. "Yep. Touring with a rock and roll band is pretty glamorous. You guys want to ride along with us to Miami?"

"You're driving all the way to Miami today?"

"Yeah, we'll have to leave around noon to get there in time for load in."

Patrick emerges from the bedroom, stretching his arms and yawning, utterly naked. Victoria screeches and then starts laughing.

"Oh, sorry. I forgot you guys were here."

He goes back in and puts on some shorts. Then there's a light knock on the door; it's Josh with two big bags of groceries. The band cooks while Victoria starts a second pot of coffee. Patrick puts the stereo on, it's like a party all of a sudden—a punk rock breakfast party. The guys in the band crack jokes constantly, and Patrick is right there with them. He's really in his element around these boys he grew up with.

At one point, Josh asks her if she and Patrick ever go camping. She's a little puzzled and says that they haven't.

"You couldn't keep him out of the woods when we were kids. We all played there, riding bikes and building forts, and later having bottle rocket wars. But he was always out there, lots of time just by himself, communing with nature or something."

After the food is gone, Josh and his crew clean everything up and then hit the road. Victoria can't remember the last time she had such a good time eating breakfast.

Just as Josh and the band ship off, the phone rings, and Vic goes to answer it. Meanwhile, Patrick turns on the television, grabs a beer from the fridge, sits down on the sofa. It was great to see his old friends, he thinks, but now that they're gone, he feels a profound void. Predictable, he supposes. He begins flipping through the channels, which reminds him of his father, depressing him further. He turns off the television and goes to the bedroom to lie down.

It amazes him how suddenly and how intensely he can feel alone, even knowing that he isn't at all alone. He has Victoria, and she's great. And he has the demigods, though they haven't exactly proven to be a blessing. That thought itself seems to conjure them up as they swirl around his head like a foggy hangover. He tries to ignore them, placing a pillow over his head. It's as if they're all talking at once, filling his head with brain noise again until he can't distinguish anything. Then a single voice rings out from the chaos. It's Victoria, calling to him from the kitchen.

"Patrick, do you have any plans for Thanksgiving?"

He takes the pillow off his head, a little disoriented. "When's that again?"

"A week from Thursday."

"Uh, nope."

"Good, my parents are coming."

Now's the time then, he knows, to come clean about that. He shoots up out of the bed. "Funny thing about that."

So he tells her that it took him a while to piece it together, but that he knows them, that for most of those several weeks when he wasn't in Birmingham, he was staying with them. The "slow to connect the dots" angle seems to work; Victoria thinks this is hilarious. Now she understands, she says, why they were asking so many odd questions about him. They'd figured it out too, or nearly did. Still laughing, she says she has to call them back and tell them.

That went better than expected, he thinks.

Chapter 23

Victoria's mother gave her a shopping list, and she's gotten everything, including the smallest turkey she could find. Her mother knows that she's a vegetarian, and has been since college, but it never seems to sink in that turkey counts as meat. Maybe she'll eat some turkey anyway, since her mother is determined to cook it. She's just gotten all the groceries put away when she hears the car pull into the driveway. Her parent come in, taking in the surroundings of her humble abode, and their facial expressions admit candidly, if tacitly, what they think about it, which is that it's rather small, same as they thought about her apartment in Birmingham. She's determined, however, not to let them make her feel small. Her father goes immediately to the sofa to sit, while her mother quickly explores the other two rooms.

"Your kitchen is so tiny. Well, I'll make due. Where's Patrick?"

"He's still at work. He'll be home soon. Oh, you can put your stuff in the bedroom. We'll stay out here on the futon."

They have a suitcase, which strikes Victoria as funny. If she were going somewhere for two nights, she'd probably just take a backpack. Difference of generations. She asks them how the traffic was coming down, and her father says it was okay. Good thing they got an early start.

With his usual impeccable timing, Patrick arrives home just as Victoria runs out of small talk. He greets her parents like old friends, shaking hands vigorously with her father and hugging her mother. He calls them Pell and Clara and asks them how things are going at the house. Clara answers that it's fine and that Mag and Penny are the only two tenants at the moment, and they can take care of themselves for a couple of days.

Her father says he has a housewarming gift for Patrick, and he goes to the bedroom to retrieve it. It's a whiskey bottle, but what's in it isn't whiskey. It's that rotgut moonshine he brews at home. Patrick seems quite excited about it though and gets two small glasses from the kitchen, correctly assuming that she and her mother will abstain.

Victoria tells Patrick to be careful with that stuff, but he shrugs it off, pouring himself a double. When she goes to bed, the bottle is half empty.

A little over an hour later, she's awakened by the sound of raised voices and stomping feet, and she sits up. She hears Patrick tell someone they're full of shit, and she hears her father telling him to calm down, and then Patrick says you calm down. Throwing on a robe and slippers, she peeks out the door to see what the hell is going on, and right about then, Patrick bursts past her into the room, knocking her into the wall with the force of the door. When she gets oriented again, she can hear him puking into the toilet. At least he made it to the bathroom this time, she thinks.

꙳

By the time Patrick gets up Thanksgiving morning, it seems everyone else has been awake for hours. They're dressed; they've already been to the grocery store for last-minute additions to the meal. Also, they all seem angry at him. He says good morning, and they mumble back at him. After a couple of minutes of silence, he pulls Victoria aside

"What's going on? Why's everybody acting so grumpy?"

"You don't remember what you did last night do you?"

He isn't even hung over, though he does reek still, after sweating out moonshine all night. The last thing he remembers was asking Victoria's parents about the lake monster that Penny (or was it Mag?) had sung about. They'd said it was some local legend that somebody had made up to increase tourism. He didn't remember anything in particular after that. Maybe something about politics, or evolution, or both.

"No, I don't. But I'm sorry for whatever I did."

"Ugh. That's awfully convenient."

She pulls away, turns her back on him. It's hard to feel guilty when you don't know what you did wrong, he thinks. The situation just agitates him. She goes into the kitchen and continues with whatever she's doing. He asks if there's anything he can do to help, and she says no. Emphatically. Jeez.

He returns to the futon and pulls the covers over his head, hoping that it's not too late to start the day over again.

꙳

They eat, and nobody says anything. Nothing about the food—neither compliments or complaints—and nothing about Patrick's weird, erratic behavior the night before. For now, she'll let him stew in the mystery. She'll fill him in later about how he was picking weird fights, just being argumentative for the sake of it—politics, philosophy, even that ridiculous story about the lake monster. He was just playing devil's advocate for any position he could hone in on. She had already gone to sleep and she woke up to his shrill, raised voice on the other side of the wall. She'd gone in and tried to intervene, and he'd called her a bitch, told her to fuck off. She'd never seen him be such an asshole. It must have been the moonshine—a complete Mr. Hyde.

In the morning, she'd talked to her parents, said he isn't usually like that. They said they were concerned for her, and for him too, and obviously still upset about it.

In an hour, the meal is done and dishes are in the dishwasher. Victoria's father comes over and gives her a hug. "Well, I think we should be getting back."

"You're going back now?"

"Yes, your mother and I think that'll be best."

"But I thought you were going back tomorrow."

"Traffic will be worse tomorrow, and we miss our regular routine."

She watches in near disbelief as they load their suitcase into the car and drive away, just like that.

Chapter 24

Hung over, in the small office at the back of the store, Patrick tries to keep his mind focused on the CD catalog in front of him—a thick volume with albums listed in small columns—and off the night before. The Thanksgiving debacle was only a few days ago, and already he's screwed up again. He takes a yellow highlighter and tentatively marks a couple of items that sound familiar to him. He has a sales report from the previous week somewhere, but he can't remember quite where he put it.

Also, his only employee, Derek, didn't show up yesterday, or the day before. Annabel from the video store is watching the CD area while he does his paperwork, and she's supposed to tell him if Derek shows up.

The night before he attended an "art event" billed as "Vomitorium." He sat at the bar smoking, watching from a bemused distance the ecstasy-addled college kids dance to the thoracic thump and drone that emanated from the speakers just above his head. Brightly colored, neo-psychedelic sculptures of phalluses towered around the dance floor. He didn't plan on staying there much longer.

But then he thought he saw Cherry Hinderson again, on the other side of the dance floor. Shortly, she was standing in front of him. "Hi Patrick. Want to see my new tattoo?"

She turned to show him a black tribal pattern across her back. "What does it mean?"

"It doesn't mean anything, at least not to me. Why does shit have to mean shit? I wouldn't want a tattoo that means something. It would be, like, too obvious to everybody what I was all about."

"OK. I hear you. So . . . how's your love life?"

"Oh, it's great. I'm a lesbian now."

They sat drinking at the bar for a long time, and then Cherry's girlfriend came over from the dance floor—a thin, pissed-off looking, black-haired woman named Fiona. She had a nose ring and a lip ring, and she wore a dark red body stocking, which did nothing to hide her erect nipples. She embraced Cherry from behind and began to nibble on her ear.

"Fiona, this is Patrick. He's a very old friend. We've known each other for years."

"He fucking you?"

"Not at the moment."

Acting jealous, Fiona stomped away.

"It isn't nice to tease her like that."

"Oh, she loves it. She'll be back. So what about it?"

"What about what?"

"Wanna fuck? I've always wanted to fuck you, but you were too shy."

"No thanks. It wasn't shyness so much as the fact that . . . well, never mind."

Again they sat for a while in silence, drinking, smoking, not looking. Cherry began fidgeting and looking very annoyed. Then suddenly she had an outburst. "Look. You're not so sexy either. It doesn't matter. Fucking is just about letting go. It's about letting yourself, like, fall back into a state of natural vulgarity. I think you're afraid to fuck me. You're afraid to see yourself go that low, to let your animal instincts take over." He didn't answer, took a drag of his cigarette, and let it out slowly, like a sigh. She continued. "I thought you would understand. You seem to understand so many things."

"What the hell does that mean?"

"I don't know. You always seem to have this, like, wisdom."

Then they drank more. The lights were spinning hallucinogenic colors, and the music pounded through the smoky air barking like the sound of sixty dogs. Fiona returned. "Ready to go home, hon?"

"Yeah. Patrick, you want to come see our place? Smoke a bowl or two?"

"Okay."

He'd followed them on his motorcycle to a duplex near downtown. Their apartment was decorated with posters of industrial bands and black curtains, which hung over all the windows, over all the doorways, and from random places on the ceiling. They put on some music, not dance music. It was ethereal, spooky sounding. A banshee-like female voice screeched in the background of the record like an offstage accident. They smoked some pot, not very good pot. It made Patrick cough. Then he sat back and listened to the strange music with his eyes closed.

Ashley, lying back on the fuzzy orange sofa smoking a ginseng cigarette. The gods have been kind to her. Her solitude. Sol. Sun. She welcomes him, forgives him, smells sweet like ginseng. Feels her hair breeze warmly across his face. Her arms around his waist. Her tongue gliding down his body. Enveloping him in her warmth.

He opened his eyes and found Cherry writhing on top of him.

Fiona was nearby masturbating on the bed. He pulled away.

"Look. I've gotta go."

"Right now?"

But he was already out the door. He told Vic he'd been too drunk to call, couldn't use his cell phone, couldn't figure it out. He's isn't sure how he's going to make it up to her, but he sincerely wants for things to work out with her. Even before this, she's wanted him to "get help," whatever that means. She's been leaving pamphlets around the apartment with titles like Are You a Sociopath? He doesn't know what his problem is. It's no clearer now than it was all those months ago when he left Lyonness.

The door of his office opens, and it's Derek, seeming to have a couple more face piercings than the last time Patrick saw him.

"Annabel told me you were back here."

"Yeah. Have a seat."

He's going to have to fire Derek. He's not quite sure how to go about it. "Do you ever think about circles?"

PART II: DOBBY

Chapter 25

Dobby wakes to the sound of a basketball bouncing on the kitchen floor and coming closer. With each collision of rubber against linoleum, his skull contracts sympathetically with the under-inflated ball, and then expands again with the springing sound that resonates through the hardwood-floor hallways. The television speaks in tongues, a howling light.

After a minute, Dobby sees Patrick there beside him, sees him moving his lips. He can't distinguish between Patrick's voice and the voice of Charity Rodgers, the young local news anchor. Both are talking quickly and erratically, or so it seems, about Martians, President Ray-gun, monkeys, detectives, gasoline, lizards, airplanes, and godknowswhatelse. All these images are swirling around him like a dreamy tornado with him as the eye.

Finally, he gets himself together enough to indicate his desire for a lower volume and a slower rate of discourse using an up-and-down gesture of his extended arm, palm toward the floor. He's spinning and soaked with sweat. He's not sure anything will come out when he opens his mouth, but he manages to say, "Turn it down to seven. And do something about that other noise."

Patrick turns off the TV Dobby sits up, wipes some drool off the front of his shirt. Things are still spinning a bit but slowing down.

"Now, what are you on about?"

Patrick's words are still blending in together. Martians, monkeys, lizards, zen, whatnot. It's apparently some kind of game or fantasy that Patrick and his friends made up. Not real. The upshot, best Dobby can tell, is that it involves some monkey detective and some space aliens. Dobby listens with wavering patience to the complex rules, the characters involved, the excitement in the boy's young voice. Zen. Just a sound, but the buzz of it stands out to him, seems familiar, but he can't place it. It all sounds foolish and crazy.

"This monkey man . . . I don't get it. Is he a monkey or a man?"

"Both. Neither. He's just Monkeyman."

"Hmph. So you're like some kind of child god, huh? Creating a world out of nothing?" Patrick seems to consider this, shrugs. Dobby suddenly remembers the time of night, and that children, at some point, need nourishment. "You eat supper?"

"Ate at Dorian's house."

"A'ight. It's getting late. Go on and get ready for bed then."

Dobby waits while the boy brushes his teeth. He can hear Patrick whispering to himself in the bathroom. "It's gonna be a'ight Bobby. We'll get that lizard before he gets us."

"Stop playin' and brush your teeth, boy."

As Patrick undresses and puts on pajamas, Dobby thinks again about this game, wonders if such fantasies are good, bad, or merely harmless for a boy his age—a boy a little old for imaginary friends. At least the boy's creative, he thinks. Really is almost a kind of god, inventing a whole absurd universe, though not much more absurd than this one really.

He goes to get himself another beer from the fridge, but before he gets it open, he hears a voice from behind the wall.

"Dad!"

Dobby puts the bottle down on the counter, trudges down the hallway and pokes his head in the door. Patrick's night light casts a jagged red glow on the wall.

"I'm scared."

"It's just shadows. Turn off that light, and it'll go away."

"No it's Harold. Bobby's scared too. Harold's trying to kill him."

"Who's Harold?"

"Giant lizard."

"Listen. There ain't nobody or nothin' in there with you. Quit playin' and go to sleep, hear?"

"Yeah."

"What?"

"Yes sir."

"That's better. Night."

"Night."

Dobby wonders where Patrick picked up the word "zen." All he knows is it's some kind of Chinese religion. Must be he heard it from Josh Abelman's dope smoking hippie parents. And who is this "Bobby" kid he keeps talking about? Never met that one, as far as he can remember. Bobby, Dobby. Funny. People who mishear his name sometimes call him Bobby, and sometimes he just doesn't feel up to correcting them.

He already regrets that he wasn't more coherent and insightful during that father/son exchange, that his mind was too muddled to form sentences out of the speckles and splinters that had entered his thoughts. He doesn't seem to have a talent for this parenting business. He has no fatherly wisdom to impart to the next generation. Every second of it exhausts him. At times, it seems like he can't possibly keep it up another day.

Once Patrick is soundly asleep, Dobby quietly steps outside and has a cigarette on the front porch. Again the unintelligible whispering begins. First, he thinks it's the boy. Leaving the cigarette burning on the railing, he steps back in and peeks into the bedroom. The boy's asleep, so he returns to the porch, and it starts again.

Against his will, his mind turns to when some of the guys from the wrestling team were teasing him and locked him in the cabinet inside the chemistry classroom. Robbie Healy again. Edwin and Kevin went along with it, though they should have stood up for him. He doesn't know how they managed to get him in there. They told him the fumes in there would get him high or something. He remembers the stale dust and that he let it all happen without resistance, and when his husky body was cramped inside that dark space, his mind was elsewhere, transcending the moment. Sometimes, these memories just sneak up on him like that, and he can't put them out of his mind. Edwin, eventually, was the one who let him out of there. He was also sweet on Sally back then. Maybe why he didn't do something sooner. Last Dobby heard of Edwin, he'd moved to Jackson and was running for some office or other.

Then it dawns on him—what the house was whispering to him. It's about the boy. It isn't his. Didn't come from him, came from someone else, somewhere else. When he married Sally, she was already pregnant, something she was in utter fantods about. They'd only done it once. But something always did disturb him about it, something vague and unknowable to him. The timing didn't seem quite right. And Sally was pious, but not immaculate.

Without a thought about what he might be doing, his feet start moving, and he begins ascending the hill that separates the residential enclave where he lives from the main road through town. The cool of the night soothes him. His worries and doubts about the boy grow more faint. Over the course of his walk, the boy himself and his childish imaginary world gradually fade from flesh to formless memories until it's not an actual boy but a voice in his conscience, a voice that asks him what he's doing here, what's his purpose, and asks him to consider these questions so that he can rise above the confines of his own mundane small town life. Dobby arrives at Mickey's—from the outside a nondescript bar with a plain wooden door. The sign outside simply says "Beer." He briefly thanks and praises the childgod for placing this watering hole in his path.

It's a weeknight, so there's not much going on inside either. There are a couple of Air Force pilots playing pool in one corner. The small stage in the back, where local boys occasionally pick guitars and banjos, is bare. A small group of regulars—mostly of a younger generation, many of them college students from nearby Tuscaloosa, which is in a dry county—hovers near the bar and around the jukebox.

He pulls a stool up to the bar, orders a domestic draft, waves politely to some vaguely familiar faces, and then begins rolling a cigarette.

"Would you mind rolling one for me?"

It's the dark-haired girl on the adjacent stool. She's dressed in a black sweater and jeans, drinking coffee, writing in a small notebook that lies open before her, and something about it strikes him as grotesque, like she's dissecting a cadaver. He looks at her dubiously. It doesn't seem very lady-like to him to smoke hand-rolled cigarettes for some reason, but what the hell. Praise the childgod that such a beauty, though a gloomy one, would even speak to him. He gives her the one he just finished constructing and lights it for her, then rolls another for himself.

"You in school?"

As she takes a drag off the cigarette, she points to the logo of a nearby community college on the front of her notebook.

"Ok, and then what?"

"Mississippi State. I'll major in History or English, I guess. Then I suppose I'll drop out after a year and travel around the country, try to get to Europe."

"You already plan to drop out after a year?"

"Many things are possible, man, but that seems likely."

Many things are possible. Praise the childgod. Somewhere inside her, Dobby sees more of the dark, murky thing in himself, the speckled splintering that eats at his pancreas and feeds the machine that shakes his nerves. He struggles to shudder it off, internally invoking the childgod and begging for respite. He takes a deep swig from his plastic cup of beer.

"I didn't go to school myself. I install electric garage door systems."

There isn't any response from her. The jukebox whirs and starts playing 'El Paso' by Marty Robbins. Restlessly, Dobby taps his fingers along with the 6/8 time, trying to think of something else to say.

"You know what? You remind me of this episode of the Beverly Hillbillies, when Jethro makes friends with a bunch of beatniks. Somehow they get the impression that he's this tremendous hepcat, and they all start following him around and calling him 'Daddio' and stuff. You ever see that one?"

"No, I don't think I ever saw that one. Listen, man . . . I'm not trying to be rude or anything, but I don't want to talk to you about that."

Clearly, she is bored now, and he is bothering her. A few more people have come in. The room begins to fill with smoke and also with her boredom. He orders another beer, allowing this to distract the both of them from each other, to break the awkward silence with a silence that is less clumsy. As he drinks, he stares forward, trying not to look at what she is writing, but he looks anyway. Immediately, he recognizes words that are unmistakably transcribed from their conversation only a couple of minutes earlier. He decides to test the waters.

"Another old show I like is the Lone Ranger. Interesting mythology behind that. Supposedly, he was this Texas Ranger, and he was well known. He was riding with a group of rangers who were attacked by bandits, and he was the sole survivor. But everybody thought he was dead. And he had to wear that little mask so nobody would recognize him. I always liked that stunt where he'd jump off a balcony and land on a horse. Seems like that'd be hell on yer nads."

"Listen, man . . ."

The second time she has said that. He wonders if she will add the "I'm not trying to be rude," but she does not.

"Don't watch much television?"

"No."

She sounds now not only bored, but exasperated. He returns his thoughts to his beer, but then he sees that she has now clearly written in her notebook the words 'Lone Ranger' and 'hell on yer nads.'

"I kind of want to be left alone now. Is that cool? Thanks for the cigarette."

"Sure . . . Sorry to bother you."

He gets up from his bar stool. The smoke in the room is beginning to burn his eyes. He should leave her alone. Her notation, making his words so concretely existent, eats at him further, and so he tears himself away. Briefly, he paces around the perimeter of the room, as if to attempt conversation on another front or check the upcoming jukebox selections. Finally he simply leaves, although "simply" is not exactly correct, because once outside, he is again directionless, and the direction he chooses is not the one that leads back to his house.

꿎

Encounter note from Bryce Hospital, CSU, Tuscaloosa, Alabama:

Patient: 15164 —John Alexander
Date: 04/12/1997
Provider: Sydney J Carrington M.D

History of present illness: John "Dobby" Alexander is a 43 year-old man who reports feeling depressed and pessimistic about the future, or brooding about the past and with no desire to continue living.

Past medical/surgical history: He reports no previous treatment for alcohol dependence or depression.

Personal history: He reports frequent beer consumption and hard liquor consumption, an inability to control the amount of alcohol consumed, and drinking alcohol regularly, and feeling guilty about it for the past 25 years. He reports no other addictions or mental health problems in his family.

Review of systems:
Systemic symptoms: a recent 20 lbs loss of weight over a 2 month time period.
Gastrointestinal symptoms: the appetite is decreased. Neurological symptoms: there is clumsiness or awkwardness of the hands and moderate concrete memory lapses or loss.

Psychological symptoms: Frequent insomnia.

Physical findings

Vital Signs	Value	Normal Range
tympanic membrane		
temperature	98.6 F	99-101
respiration rate	18 per min	18 -26
pulse rate	62 bpm	50 -100
blood pressure		
while sitting	130/75 mmHg	96-140/60-90
weight	170 lbs	123 -215
height	69 in	64 -73

General appearance: The patient appears uncomfortable, nervous, exhausted, and poorly hydrated.

Psychological: There is moderate psychomotor retardation, impulsivity, nail biting, grinding of the teeth, odd and eccentric speech, negativism, decreased eye-to-eye contact, the speech rate is slowed, and the affect is flat. The estimated intelligence is high.

Assessment
1. Alcohol dependence with dementia;
2. Major depression, single episode.

Plan
1. 5 days mandatory psychiatric therapy in-patient for ETOH w/ detox;

Sydney J Carrington M.D.

Another town, another year going by, another smoky bar seems like home. Dobby's been in St. Louis a couple of weeks now, traveling upstream. He wonders what a guy named Louis could do to deserve sainthood. Not a very saintly-sounding name, if you ask him. Drunk, he sits at a corner table scribbling furiously in a spiral bound notebook, whiskey on the rocks firmly gripped by the hand that does not write. His pen hand can barely keep pace with his muse. In the cobwebbed corners of his solipsism, translucent grains of dust transmigrate into stars sprinkled across the night. The land below is flat and decayed, endowed by a neglectful childish creator, inhabited by dark oily creatures— conflations of mythologies, fantasies and psychic disturbances that have congealed and solidified and developed voices. He is merely a medium for the voices that spin around him in swift but graceful laps. As they speak, he transcribes in a frenetic pinched hand, a habit he picked up years before in another bar, in another town— he doesn't remember where or when.

A deep blue neon river springs from the voices, adding shape and color to the words, words that tell stories of revolutions, rock music, and space aliens. Old Scratch, Old Cloven-hoof, Old Odysseus, Old Man Moses would appreciate this, would bathe in it, but it is the childgod and his band of demigods who will read fortunes in the silt.

"... Sometimes I'm dancing, and I don't even realize that I'm dancing ..."

A clamor of quarters, kerchunked into the belly of the pool table introduces the familiar clacking of the billiard balls.

"... I am nothing but a poet and a whore, and I am a poor poet ..."

"... Hi Tom, nice to see you ..."

"... Happy New Year ..."

"... Cheers ..."

It's still the early evening, so Dick Clark isn't on yet. On the silent television, there's a documentary about the Loch Ness Monster, narrated by subtitle. On the other side of the pool table, a group of men discuss details of Christ's famous death scene. Across the bar, another group of men discusses football. Lots of men like to discuss things like football, Christ, Nessie, whiskey. He can do without the football discussion, and he can't make out even what they're really saying about it, so his attention turns again to the television.

REPORTS OF SONAR OBJECTS AT LEAST FIFTEEN FEET LONG HAVE PERSISTED FOR THE PAST TEN YEARS.

". . . It's hard to say exactly what it was . . ."
". . . His death was quicker than most because they cut him. It took most of them four or five days to die, but they cut him, and he died quickly . . ."

SOME RESEARCHERS RESORTED TO OUTRIGHT FRAUD.

He is piss drunk and totally free, for the moment, from the confines of his inner dialog. The jukebox whirs and spits, zenzenzenzen, a motorcycle throttle; the bend of a whammy bar on an overdriven electric guitar breaks into a frenzied drumbeat. The deep vibrations stir him to move. He drains the last drops of bourbon from his glass and approaches the bar. Where once there was a redheaded Irish bartender, there is now a man-sized lizard with blood red skin wiping the counter surface with a stained white rag. Dobby is accustomed to this. For the last couple of years, all bartenders become this beast after a few rounds. And the old men at the bar become large apes, grizzly chimpanzees and brash orangutans grunting and screeching at each other in their various primate languages.

Dobby holds up one finger, and the lizard silently fills another small glass with ice and whiskey. The television is changed to news. Chastity Rodgers discusses Clinton's blowjobs with a mild smirk, cuts to dyspeptic Republican senators. Then she discusses chaos in Kosovo. There is footage.

Dobby puts a five on the counter and takes the glass with a warm 'preciate it, very careful not to let his shaky hands spill, just in time before a group of idiotic baboons crowding into his area of the bar get themselves whipped into a frenzy over the picketers on the tube getting their skulls smashed in by police. The brutal scene temporarily distracts Dobby from his thoughts and his work, but he turns away from the beasts, both those at the bar and those on the tube, and continues his literary mission. He is lucid enough to know that this world is not the one in which other men live, and he has vowed to capture as much of it as he is capable on the page. For what purpose, he could not say. It has been predestined. Praise the childgod and his ever-expanding labyrinth.

The deeper he explores into this wasteland, the more closed in and small it becomes for him. In the beginning, he himself was childlike. It was his own personal epic, where he discovered the relics of a past civilization in the deserted plains, meeting the strange and frightening creatures that inhabit the darkness. Every man, he thinks, seeks the thrill of exploration, new frontiers, and these are frontiers that no one else has ever seen, will ever see. These pathways and corridors, barren plains and cloistral tunnels, belong only to the realm of Dobby, not belonging to him or created by him, but seen, touched, smelled and tasted by only him, and of course, this is exciting, to a degree. Lately, and tonight in particular, he is tired.

For so many years, years he couldn't count, he has traveled, searching sometimes for a simple door, hoping to find the reckless boy, from whose loins all this expanse emerged so that he can understand how he came to be here and how he can get out. Dobby has no real memory of ever seeing this boy, but he knows of him. He has seen visions of him casually casting his spells while bouncing a rubber ball off the ground. He has figured out that there is a psychic connection between himself and the boy. Dobby wonders if the boy, wherever he may be, knows this also.

In a similar psychic fashion, he's aware of a more remote mastermind, something strange, even alien who, in the absence of the boy, rules over the nothingness through which Dobby slogs. By ineptness or carelessness, the once rich resources left behind by the creator, the childgod, have now been squandered by this two-headed, green skinned monster that commands the armies of apes and whose lizard-like servants tend to the far spread oases where Dobby stops to document his experience and quench his thirst.

As Dobby writes, the walls, ceiling and floor gradually mutate, spread out and become cruciform wings of a massive baroque cathedral, marble cherubs winking at him from the transepts. The electric glow that came from above the bar transforms into an arched window of stained glass, and the violent conflict that had previously been a mere electronic image now occurs in life-sized silhouette on the pane. He can hear the clashing rocks, sticks and flesh even over the jukebox to his back, now a grand organ, ringing out a processional hymn. The bar is now a chancel rail, where the reptilian deacon helps to prepare the sacrament for the simian parish. Although Dobby is no stranger to the inexplicable and horrific, this is new, and his body stiffens from terror.

". . . You alright, there buddy. You don't look too well."

The clamor outside grows, and the doors burst open, what remains of the sun on the western horizon highlighting an edge around the dark intruders. Seven shadowy figures huddled together in the doorway, and not one with a recognizable feature. Dobby squints to try to see if they have faces, but all he sees is the homogenous shape lingering there, ecliptic, blocking the exit. After an eternal moment, they enter, followed by a second similar group and then a third. And then, as quickly as the rain stops, he is in a bar once again, too much in the way of the crowds to be anymore anonymous.

He drinks the last of his drink, packs his notebook neatly into the army green denim backpack he carries and rises to leave.

Encounter note from United Hospital, CSU, St. Paul, Minnesota:

Patient: 12183 – John Alexander
Date: 04/12/2007
Provider: Roger Ford M.D

History of present illness: Mr. Alexander is a 53 year-old man who reports feeling depressed and pessimistic about the future, or brooding about the past and no desire to continue living.

Past medical/surgical history: He reports numerous previous treatments for alcohol dependence and depression, beginning 10 years ago. Most recent hospitalization was 4 years ago.

Personal history: He reports frequent hard liquor consumption, an inability to control the amount of alcohol consumed, and drinking alcohol regularly, and feeling guilty about it for the past 30 years. He reports that his brother is addicted to heroin and that his mother suffered a series of "nervous breakdowns" before she died.

Review of systems:
Systemic symptoms: a recent 20 lbs loss of weight over a 1 month time period.
Gastrointestinal symptoms: the appetite is decreased.

Neurological symptoms: there is clumsiness or awkwardness of the hands and severe concrete memory lapses or loss. The patient claims to have been born in the city of "Zen, Mississippi." There appears to be no such place.

Psychological symptoms: Terminal insomnia and feeling nervous or anxious.

Physical findings

Vital Signs	Value	Normal Range
tympanic membrane temperature	98.6 F	99 ⁻101
respiration rate	21 per min	18 ⁻26
pulse rate	59 bpm	50 ⁻100
blood pressure while sitting	135/75 mmHg	96-140/60-90
weight	150 lbs	123 ⁻215
height	69 in	64 ⁻73

General appearance: The patient appears nervous, acutely exhausted, and poorly hydrated.

Psychological: There is severe psychomotor retardation, impulsivity, nail biting, grinding of the teeth, odd and eccentric speech, negativism, decreased eye-to-eye contact, the speech rate is slowed, and the affect is flat. The estimated intelligence is high. There is suicidal ideation. The patient claims to fantasize about being "crushed underneath a church," and appears to believe he can cause this to happen via "telekinesis."

Assessment
1. Alcohol dependence with dementia;
2. Major depression, multiple episodes.

Plan

1. 5 days mandatory psychiatric therapy in-patient for ETOH w/ detox;

2. Recommended 28 days rehab

Roger Ford M.D.

❧

A howling light rushes in through the sliver of a window above and then vanishes as suddenly as it arrived. Dobby is curled up in a corner of the church basement, shivering, dizzy and nauseated. The shadows make judging, snarling faces at him, monstrous faces. He tries to concentrate on a prayer, serenity, courage. He can't get through a full incantation of it without images bursting into his mind of the walls and ceiling collapsing in on him, a laughing childgod in the distance.

The courage to change the things he can. He manages to stand up, stumble into the dark, empty hallway and into a doorway. He leans on a wall, and it feels cool on his back. As his eyes adjust, the wall opposite him, only three or four feet away, bulges out toward him, its red tiles forming into scales that cascade downward into a tail.

He rushes down to the end of the hallway. There's a screeching in his skull, an itching all over. There's a set of stairs and a door, but it's locked. Dead end. Everything closing in. The slightest glint catches his eye at the other end, if only he can get himself there. He puts one foot forward, then the other. Feels like walking through a morass of sewage, but that little bit of light seems attainable.

He begins to feel like he doesn't remember how to breathe, lets out a yelp, runs toward another set of steps, ascends.

He pushes through the doorway, and he's in an open room, partially lit by streetlamps just outside. The sensation overwhelms him that he needs air, needs to get outside. Can't go back downstairs to the window that let him in, though, because there's something deeply wrong down there.

He tries a door, but it won't budge. Windows won't open either. Another hallway, another stairway. An open window. The sky. He keeps ascending, rushing forward—his life, his regrets, chasing him close behind.

Everything turns.

PART III: A MOMENT OF SILENCE

Chapter 26

There's a flapping and a thunk in the dark, then more flapping. Munford Coldwater opens his eyes, slowly makes note of the time—3:12 am. The overfed creamsicle tabby, Captain Fancy Pants, also seems to hear the sound, leaps over Munford's belly and circles around to nuzzle open the bedroom door.

Munford switches on the living room light, twists and tucks the stretched-out elastic of his white briefs to keep them from sliding down. A bird flutters around near the ceiling, absurdly slapping itself against the bookshelves. The intruder knocks over a couple of perilously perched photo frames, spilling over a narrow plastic flower vase and the arrangement of late-blooming aromatic aster and rose verbena that Munford picked from the yard the day before. Captain Fancy Pants hides under the sofa. Munford locates a cardboard shoebox (Adidas running shoes, size 9 1/2, white, which he wears when working in his garden) to trap the bird. He sneaks up on it, covering it with the box, and then he carefully scoots it out the front door, releasing it into the brisk Mississippi air.

As soon as he comes back inside, however, another bird swoops down out of the fireplace, smacking itself against the walls repeatedly until it runs out of strength and alights behind a curtain. Yet another bird descends out of the fireplace, then another. Could be chimney swifts, he thinks. The birds' manic gesticulations around the living room and adjoining kitchen disperse splotches of soot on the walls and floor. With some of the ash knocked away he can see that they aren't swifts. The distinctive chirping is the final clue he needs to identify the birds as house sparrows. Why they were in his chimney, he cannot guess. He can hear the description of the birds in the voice of his now-dead grandmother Audra May reading from her *Encyclopedia of Southeastern Ornithology*, which was so enormous in her lap that it spanned over the arms of her wheelchair. Audra May and her alcoholic daughter Edna, Munford's aunt, used to refer to this tome frequently and bicker about the subtle differences between various species indigenous to the area.

The Captain creeps out to inspect one of the sparrows, which is trapped behind a bulky oak writing desk that belonged to Munford's great uncle Zeke. Munford grabs the cat, tosses him into the bedroom and closes the door. He scrambles frantically around the room with his shoebox, moving furniture away from the walls, and sliding the shoebox across the floor and out onto the porch for release. Captain Fancy Pants yowls from the next room as birds continue to invade, flutter, and bump around in a spastic spree. Each time Munford thinks he has ousted the last sparrow, he hears peeping from behind a piece of furniture.

Finally, he strips down another, larger cardboard box and tapes it over the fireplace to prevent more disturbances. He has only about an hour to sleep before he has to get up and go to work.

For that hour, he remains supine on the thin, lumpy mattress and stares alternately at the ceiling fan and the backs of his eyelids. The foreboding overture of a sinister symphony resounds within his eardrums, vigorously orchestrated and conducted by his heart at a steady tempo of 90 beats per minute. His gut feels acidic and heavy with gas, occasionally accenting the biological magnum opus with its rumbles and emissions.

The Captain sleeps undisturbed in the crevice between Munford and the wall.

At 5 a.m., Munford forces himself out of the bed, dons a pair of old but clean blue jeans and a light yellow, short-sleeved button-down that Aunt Edna gave him the last Christmas she was alive. Outside, it's a cold and foggy November morning, so he also puts on a heavy brown coat that he bought from the church's charity thrift store a few weeks ago.

He begins the ten-block walk to the Lyonness Episcopal Church of the Incarnation, where he works as the sexton. He talked his way into the job two years ago, soon after he inherited the home where he'd spent his summers as a boy, after the tragic automobile accident in which the Almighty hand swept Edna, Audrey May and Zeke swiftly and mercifully away. With his parents both long buried in Tupelo, a bitter divorce, and retirement with a pension from twenty years as a reporter at *The Tupelo Daily Journal*, he had nothing keeping him from retreating to country life in a familiar small town. He likes the work, and it gives him something to do with his time.

As he walks, he makes a mental list of the jobs he needs to complete before he can go home and try to catch up on his sleep: his weekly ritual of walking through the labyrinthine corridors, locking and unlocking doors, adjusting the temperature. There's also a window that needs repair in one of the old Sunday School classrooms they don't use anymore. The latch is broken, and the window can be pulled open from the outside. Security isn't a major concern for most people in the little town of Lyonness, but there's no use taking unnecessary chances.

Since it's his duty to open the church, he is always the first to arrive on Sundays. In addition, this particular Sunday, he is obliged to arrive an hour earlier than usual to help prepare for the monthly Sidewalk Breakfast, which is not actually held on the sidewalk, but in the Parish Hall. For these monthly events, volunteers from the church serve donated food to the homeless. Unlike the homeless in Tupelo, Jackson, Birmingham or Memphis, the homeless in Lyonness are not faceless, anonymous drifters. They are generally known by at least a few people in the church. Nonetheless, the members of the lay council have mandated the Sidewalk Breakfast to begin early because they want the homeless to be out of sight before 7:00 when people begin arriving for the early service.

As he turns down St. Andrews Street, he can just begin to see the stone brick structure of the church a couple of blocks away through the thick morning fog. Something is spread on the sidewalk in front of the church doors. First, he thinks it might be a pile of clothes. He approaches with the intention of delivering them to the charity thrift store, the proper channel for donations of that kind. As he quickens his pace, the dark bitter stench of dried blood and the appearance of crustaceal fingers peeking out from a coat sleeve verify that the eyesore is human, lying face-down on the concrete.

Thinking the person may be passed out from drunkenness, he kicks the sole of the individual's army boot, worn thin enough that a dirty gray sock peeks through at the heel. Nothing happens. Then he recognizes the person, or body of a person, rather, from previous Sidewalk Breakfasts. He's heard people, Sally Alexander for one, call the man Dobby, but he can't think of any time he's spoken to him himself. Dobby isn't moving, and Munford instantly becomes sick with himself over that kick.

He's almost certain Dobby isn't breathing, but he puts his

hand on Dobby's back, feels no air coming in. No pulse on the wrist. The face is firmly planted in the sidewalk, and there's no point in moving it. He rifles through the heavy and crowded key ring on his belt loop and finds the one to open the office door, then hurries inside and telephones for assistance. After hanging up the phone, that brief rush of adrenaline subsides, and he gets a chill, which reminds him to turn on the heat. Alone in the small office, he notices some typed, stapled pages on the secretary's desk titled "A Brief History of the Lyonness Episcopal Church of the Incarnation—Draft." Instinctively, he starts reading it, almost forgetting himself, until he hears the sirens outside a moment later.

Munford folds the pages and puts them in his pocket to copy edit later. It's still a little dark out, and the blue light on the Sheriff's car swirls with the red lights of the ambulance, washing over the couple of neighbors who have come out in bathrobes.

In front of the great, carved wood doors of the cathedral, Munford explains to a sheriff's deputy named Travis that he recognizes the man from previous Sidewalk Breakfasts and that the man goes by the name Dobby. And that's all he knows about him, it, the body.

"A'ight, Mr. Coldwater," Travis says. "Thanks for your help."

Travis is lean and lanky, like a man made of tight-wound steel wire. In his sleepy drawl, Travis tells Munford they think Dobby might have jumped off the roof. Or maybe he fell.

"That don't make much sense," Munford says. "He was an old man. How'd he get up there?"

"Ain't my job to figure out how he got up there. The severity of the contusions on the facial area and the position of the body evidences a fall. No indication of foul play. That's that, far as I'm concerned. The coroner'll back me up, I reckon. If not, we'll pick up where we left off."

Munford still finds this situation puzzling, but he leaves the EMT team to their tasks, and he returns to his own. He unlocks the front doors. Normally, he would have propped them open, but he decides to wait. He enters the vestibule and closes the door behind him. He looks up and over his shoulder at the Incarnation in stained glass. The angel stands over Mary in a circle of golden light. How perfectly the artist managed to capture Mary's look of horror and astonishment and wonder.

He continues through the chapel to the small door behind the chancel that leads to a narrow hallway in the administrative building. He unlocks that door and makes his way back by the rectory and office. He opens the main entrance to the Parish Hall and then the back entrance. He unlocks the door of the Sunday School building, then turns the handle on the yellow door that leads downstairs, only to find that it's already unlocked. He puzzles over this a moment, then assumes he had forgotten to lock it the previous week. It's an easy door to forget about.

In the basement of the Sunday School building is an area that the old people in the congregation jokingly call the "catacombs," consisting of some old classrooms now used only for storage and a long underground passage that connects these rooms to a staircase leading into the choir booth inside the chapel. This allows the choir members to walk en masse from the choir room, which is located in the Sunday School building, directly to the front of the chancel, where they sit during services.

In the quiet isolation and darkness of this virtually unused floor, Munford reflects, safe from the imminent company of any arriving parishioners. Can't believe I kicked him, he mumbles. The words rumble through the cold natural reverb of the hallway tiles. A plane of natural light on a downward sloping axis, emitted through a classroom with an open door on Munford's left side, illuminates his dead man kicking shoes as they tick across the floor.

At the end of the hallway, he re-enters the chapel through the choir booth and returns to the front doors just in time for Dobby's departure in the ambulance. Travis is still sitting in his car, taking notes. Reverend Healey parks behind him in his black Corvette, leaps out and heads straight up to Munford.

"What happened here?"

The rector's voice is booming. It isn't difficult to imagine that the words he speaks in his sermons are truly the word of God. And his thick, six-and-a-half-foot frame, that of a former Crimson Tide half-back, invokes an authority that few ever found cause to question.

"Looks like somebody, a homeless fella, um, somehow got on top of the roof, and took the short way back down. Fella went by the name Dobby."

Munford sees the Reverend's round red face drain of color. Munford tells him that the fall was fatal, and that Travis is pretty sure nobody else was involved. Without another word, Healy turns and enters the church. Munford follows, tortured by the silence, hoping for advice or spiritual wisdom of some sort. The Reverend bows slowly and solemnly before he passes the altar, then ducks through the low doorway behind the chancel. The rectory door closes with a gentle, barely audible tick.

Confused and still haunted by the sound of his own footsteps, Munford continues down the hallway to the Parish Hall. There, Martha Healy, the Reverend's wife, fills the oversized coffee urn. She sings a "good morning" without looking toward him. He manages to squeeze a "morning" back to her before turning his head toward the homeless, who are beginning to file into the Parish Hall through the back doors—the one that opens to the parking lot. The homeless are always herded in this way, a fact that Munford never finds exactly comfortable with his sensibilities.

Sally Alexander prepares the buffet of day-old pastries from the Rollins Bakery and some casserole-like dish that Munford can't quite identify from where he's standing. Looks like they also have pancakes and bacon. The homeless are quick to fill their plates, but take their time consuming the fare. There are maybe ten of them, all but two men, all but one black, seated around the long tables.

Sally looks pretty, as she always does, though she's dressed very modestly in a sweatshirt and loose jeans. She's a classic, buxom, pale-skinned Irish redhead, just the type he'd go for if he were just a little younger. Sally says she heard sirens earlier when she drove up and what was that all about. He puts his hand on her shoulder and fills her in. He refers to Dobby as "one of your people," which he then feels weird about having said, not really sure what he meant by it. Afterward, he's overcome by a wave of irrational and unfocused guilt and quietly slips out the back door.

To the left of the stairs that descend into the parking lot, there's a large wooden crate, which Munford has intended to clean out for a long time. He creaks it open, fans the dust away from his eyes, and starts clearing out the contents: a green, turtle shaped kiddy pool, a couple of garbage bags full of godknowswhat, a paint can, a broken umbrella, some empty cigarette packages, and several plastic forks. Crushed on the bottom are two or three more ruined kiddy pools. What he's looking for, a carefully coiled green rubber hose is tucked down the side—unused since the church installed a new sprinkler system three years ago.

Around the corner, behind the tall shrubs in the memorial garden, there's a spigot. He attaches the end of the hose to this and then methodically unrolls it as he walks past the St. Francis birdbath toward the front door of the cathedral. He places the mouth of the hose on the ground near the dried blood of Dobby on the sidewalk then returns to turn on the water.

Dead? A blank feeling comes over Sally. Dobby's being around these last three months has been so disorienting to start with, and now this. She must have looked like she was taking it hard because Munford had put his hand on her shoulder, and she resisted the impulse to fidget. The news was rather shocking, but more than grief, she feels motivated now to make this Sidewalk Breakfast an especially memorable one. She sort of chants to herself, cheers herself on—Sally doesn't dally. The donated food for this morning's breakfast was severely disappointing: the usual bag of day-old breads and muffins from Rollins Bakery, and the same bland casserole that Martha Healy makes and brings with her to the breakfast every month. That's all. Even the delivery from Rollins seems less substantial than usual, and that casserole thing . . . she doesn't understand how anyone could eat that stuff.

Sally forges into the reserves of the refrigerator, finding enough bacon and sausage to feed a marching band, as well as a couple of gallons of milk. Continuing her search, she comes across a nearly full box of pancake mix. She digs a griddle out from the cabinet, sets it on top of the stove and turns on the heat. She lays down a dozen strips of bacon and then starts mixing up pancake batter. Martha comes in to retrieve more Styrofoam coffee cups. The homeless drink a lot of coffee.

"I'll be. It sure smells wonderful in here. You're making pancakes? And bacon?"

"Yes, ma'am. And sausage."

Martha's face shrinks. "How ambitious! Who bought it?"

Sally scoops a couple of fresh hotcakes onto a serving platter and begins pouring new ones onto the griddle. "I don't know. It was in the fridge."

"Well, then I am reasonably certain it was purchased by the Episcopal Lay Council, and it is intended for the Parish Pancake Breakfast after the early service today."

Startled by Martha's accusatory tone, Sally looks up from her cooking for the first time since Martha came in to the kitchen. "What are you saying?"

"That food is not meant for the Sidewalk Breakfast. It's for the parishioners."

"Oh, come off it . . . Some of these people haven't eaten in days. There was nothing else here except a bag of old bread from Rollins and your . . . whatever that is."

"Well, what will we eat for the pancake breakfast, Sally?"

"Oh, for . . . There's plenty here for everybody, and pancake mix is cheap. If it will make you feel any better, I will go to the store during the service and replace whatever I have used. Is that okay with you?"

Martha smoothes the ruffles in her light blue flower print dress and promptly leaves the room.

A few minutes later, the food is ready. Sally brings the trays of pancakes, sausage and bacon out to the homeless, and several of them actually cheer. Now that she can rest, she returns to the kitchen and sits down on the metal footstool to think. She remembers that when Dobby came back to town, it was the previous August, a week of cantankerous heat. It was a slow Tuesday at the town's small, underappreciated library where she works four days a week. She saw him walk in, looking so strange and small and wrinkled and his hair had turned purple-gray, and she wasn't sure it was really him at first. She'd never seen him with a full beard before either. She remembers trying not to stare, turning her back and shuffling through the card catalog as if she was looking for something important, and then all of a sudden he was right there in front of her, claiming to look for a restroom or some such. It was definitely him, and the years hadn't treated him well. He wasn't the same man he once had been, even if he hadn't exactly been Prince Charming in the first place.

When he came close, she could see the familiar facial expressions that used to lie to her, and she'd found it difficult to maintain her usual reserve. His eyes were bloodshot. His body was emaciated, and he shivered, though he was wearing that tattered green trench coat in the hottest month of the year.

"I thought that was you, Dobby. What brings you back here?"

"Back? I live here. I've always been here."

"You son of a bastard bitch. Where the hell have you been for twenty years?"

"Twenty years?"

"Did you forget about our son? Did you forget about everything?"

She felt so maudlin, about to burst into tears. Their son, or hers at least. Theirs, until Dobby ran off, even if . . . There was a chance . . . well, she didn't like to think about that . . . Patrick is their son.

"Naw, ma'am, you got me confused for someone else." His manner was earnest, resolved and calm, surprisingly so. She was agitated. He wouldn't make eye contact with her. He bit at his finger calluses.

"Well, that's convenient, ain't it? I think you should probably leave."

"A'ight."

With the tacit deference of one who's used to being asked to leave places and doesn't want any trouble, he slipped quietly out the door.

A couple of days later, she saw Dobby standing outside the grocery store, ashen as a residue and thin as a rail, smoking the same damn hand-rolled cigarettes that he used to fall asleep with still burning on their sofa twenty years ago. Just standing there, he was. It suddenly occurred to her then that he was back. Really back. Not just making a brief, disturbing, ghostly appearance and going away, not making it something she could go home and try to forget about. He was here, standing there in the flesh. She marched up to him. "How long are you planning to stay in town?"

She felt like she was attacking, as she damn well had a right to, but he remained flat, didn't look at her, shrugged. "Don't know. Maybe until I die."

"Well, I hope that's soon."

He didn't respond. She tried to move in front of him, forcing a gaze, staring him down, but he continued to look up at the sky or down at the ground, anywhere but at her. She took off her glasses and rubbed her eyes.

"Where . . . where are you staying?"

"Can't say."

With tight-lipped resolve, she turned away and entered the store. When she returned with her groceries, he was gone. No surprise.

Twenty years he'd been gone, and then came back for barely an instant. She recalls how she'd been resentful for a little while. She hasn't thought about it in a long time. She is not one of those women on daytime television who suffer their whole lives because some man abandoned them. Anyway, she had already kicked him out by the time he disappeared. But he did abandon Patrick, and in the worst sort of way, sneaking out in the middle of the night. It was days before anyone could figure out what happened. Next thing she knew, she got a call that he'd been arrested for attacking the mascot at a football game and that he was being held for ten days for psychological evaluation, and then he spent 28 days in detox and rehab.

She feels a slight nausea, like post purge not sure when it's going to hit you again kind of nausea. She can barely take the smell of that casserole stuff. She looks around at the pancake batter and bacon grease splatter. Well, she thinks and perhaps says out loud, I got work to do. I better have me a cup of coffee. Sally does not dally.

She realizes, not for the first time but with more acuity, that when they were together, she cleaned the house compulsively. She scrubbed, vacuumed, swept, dusted, anything to keep her from doing any emotional work, the real woman's work she needed to do, to face up to him, address issues. She'd eventually told him to either get himself together or get out, and he got out. She was surprised at first, but he told her he knew he had problems and that he was working on them. She gave him the benefit of the doubt. It's the only thing she ever regretted giving him.

By now, the kitchen is once again spotless. She peeks out the door and sees that the homeless are no longer seated sporadically throughout the Parish Hall. She picks up the paper plates, plastic utensils and styrofoam cups, wipes down the tables. Martha and her casserole dish are already gone, which reminds her (damn) she still has to go to the store; it's just a few blocks away, as everything in Lyonness is, but as Patrick says sometimes, the town is bigger than it seems.

Young Daniel Birch wanders through the lobby and hallways of the church building looking for something to do. His parents are busy meeting with their Bible study group, which normally coincides with his Sunday School class. But his class, the third and fourth graders, got out early today. He's been previously instructed to wait on the playground when these circumstances occur, but before he gets there, he sees the yellow door. And when he sees the yellow door on this Sunday midmorning, he notes that he has never seen that yellow door open and that he doesn't have any earthly idea what's on the other side of it.

The door opens to a dark set of downward stairs, which he of course follows. The stairs at first appear to end merely at a wall, which he blindly inspects until he locates a light switch. When the fluorescent lights flicker on, he turns around, and he realizes that the stairwell opens into a hallway. Now Daniel remembers having heard there were some old Sunday School classrooms in the basement that aren't used anymore. His parents and other old folks in the church call it the catacombs. To the adults, perhaps, there is nothing special here. However, Daniel might as well have discovered the tomb of an ancient pharaoh (he's recently become fascinated by ancient Egypt, and he has been reading about the pyramids). As he imagines any archeologist would, he makes a cursory check of each room before studying any of them in great detail.

The five classrooms, three on one side of the hall and two on the other, are roughly identical, except that the two rooms on the right side of the hall have no windows, which he finds a little eerie. There are no desks or chairs, except a few broken ones piled in the far corners of each room. Between the two rooms on the right, there's a storage closet and a bathroom. He cautiously opens the door of the closet, but quickly sees that it contains only a water heater and some cobwebs. The bathroom is just a bathroom. Nothing interesting there.

The end of the hallway angles around to another long dark corridor, this one without rooms on the side. He decides to return to the classrooms before checking that out. In the first room, he flicks on the lights, which, like their counterparts in the hall, hesitate before illuminating the room with a gouty halo. He examines the chalkboard, dusted in cuneiform shadows of chalk ash that only hint of words—some Biblical and some secular, some elusive and coy. Among the runes he's able to interpret: "Samson and Delilah," "Mrs. Gangnagel" (that's his teacher—she must be even older than he thought), "Golden Calf," and "ZoSo." On the bulletin boards, he finds brittle coloring book pages of blue and green Jesuses, bordered by decades-old streamers. In a coat closet, he finds cardboard boxes of holiday decorations, including Valentines—some written upon and others unused.

He turns off the light in that room and begins to search a room across the hall. The light from the window, which is unusually close to the ceiling, is enough for him to see his way around. This room's bulletin board is filled with pairs of paper animals lined up to enter an ark barely big enough for even the pair of pink elephants near the front of the queue. The window is high on the wall, and he can't quite tell what's on the other side, so he climbs up on a short, wide bookshelf to get a better look. When he gets to the top, he sees that the window is at the ground level, but all he can see on the other side is the backside of some shrubbery.

Squinting his eyes and leaning on the window to see what's on the other side of the bushes, he gets a start when the window slides forward and opens. He can now hear the familiar squeals of his peers, and he knows that it's the playground on the other side. He pulls the window closed and jumps off the bookshelf. His landing echoes though the empty hall, and he decides he should probably leave soon. First though, he takes a minute to poke around in another cardboard box, one that he sees on the ground in the corner of the room. There's nothing in it but some notebooks full of tiny cursive writing, a couple of pens and a near-empty bottle of something labeled Old Crow that smells to him like turpentine.

Quickly flipping through a notebook, he finds one page containing a crude drawing of a dragon or maybe a lizard. Around the dragon, there's a series of concentric circles, some filled in with illegible scribble. Thinking he'd like to inspect it more thoroughly later, he tears out the page and stuffs it in his pocket. Then he decides to leave. He wants to see what was down that other hallway before he gives up his adventure, but he hears footsteps coming from down there, so he goes back out the way he came in. That'll have to wait until next week.

Begrudgingly, he walks out to the playground where he's supposed to meet his parents. He notes the row of bushes next to the building and looks to see if he can find the unlocked window again. It isn't hard to locate, and he could easily open it from the outside. He thinks that he could probably get into the room from outside by sliding into the window on his stomach and then stepping onto the bookshelf. He knows better than to try it in his Sunday clothes, though, and anyway he hears his mother calling him from the steps. He walks to the far end of the row of bushes before stepping out in the open so that he can conceal his point of origin as much as possible.

When his mother asks him where he's been he says around the corner, and thankfully, she asks for no further explanation. Without another word, the three of them, he, his mother and father, walk to the car, and he climbs into the back seat.

"What I don't understand . . . is how he got up there."

"Terrance, let's not talk about this now."

From where he sits, behind his father, Daniel can see his mother gesturing towards him from the front seat.

"OK, I'm just saying . . ."

"How who got up where?"

"See, I told you . . . Nothing, Hon. It's just some boring grown-up stuff."

"Now, Nancy, let's not pussyfoot around this. He's probably heard something anyway. Did your teacher say anything to you about the accident this morning?"

"No, what happened?"

"She probably hadn't heard yet. They only told us after the service."

"Poor Sally . . ."

"Heard what? What happened to Mrs. Alexander?"

"Listen, son. We'll talk about this when we get home. Do you want to stop and get lunch?"

"Sure."

∽

At home, Reverend Healy reviews with a cigarette the day that has just passed. The sun is half down, bathing him in an amber haze. There are no birds outside. The girls are getting ready for bed. Dobby is dead. Healy exhales, watches the smoke trickle through the window screen into that evening sun, which sinks behind the bold green hills and pastures that surround his home.

An antique clock on the wall behind him marks the quarter after the hour. After two long, considered drags, he carefully places the burning butt on a tin ashtray on the windowsill. To keep the smoke blowing outside, he turns on a small fan on the bookshelf.

He hadn't heard old Dobby's name in maybe twenty years. Nobody told him Dobby had returned to the community, in whatever shape it was he managed to take on. Homeless, no less. For some of the creatures in this world, though, it is a challenge to find even an ounce of love in your heart. But . . . Love the sinner; hate the sin. He's in God's hands now.

Poor old Sally. It's no wonder at all that her boy turned out to have a rebellious streak. He hasn't seen that kid in years either, come to think of it. Like father like son, he imagines. The boy really didn't have much of a chance, though the Reverend recalls that he tried at the time to reach out to him. Thought he was too intelligent for religion or some such. Love the sinner, et cetera.

Good thing he was there for her when all that happened, when Dobby disappeared on her and Sally came to him all flustered and directionless, those giant brown eyes soaking and red. He supposes he helped her in more ways than one, made her feel like a real woman for the first time in a long while. Nothing wrong with it, far as he's concerned, being a human man after all. Was before he met Martha, of course, married her and adopted Yennie and Li. Sally sure was a firecracker, though, he thinks, feels hard as a rock just thinking about it. He taps his erection with his fist then slowly, almost reluctantly, makes his way to the oak desk across the room.

He sits in front of his computer screen, forms a pyramid with his elbows on his desk and slowly plants his chin into the palms of his hands, the archival version of sermon he delivered earlier today still missing the edits he made on the fly this morning. For the sake of posterity, he corrects some typos and rewords a few phrases here and there. He'll post it to his website later in the week.

This week is the last Sunday in the period we call "the Season after Pentecost" or "Ordinary Time," the time when we concentrate on various aspects of the faith, and especially the role of the church in the world.

Our observance of the Christian seasons and festivals can become an important tool for education and discipleship in the faith, as well as a vehicle for spiritual growth and vitality. And now as we prepare to begin the church year anew, we take time to reflect on the role we, as Christians, play in the modern world.

Kind of boilerplate stuff he thinks. He probably put most of them to sleep with it. He'd considered changing the whole thing and talking extemporaneously about Dobby instead. Ultimately, though, the thought of speaking off the top of his head worried him too much. Before he got started on the formal part of the sermon, he mentioned the incident as delicately as he could; asking for a moment of silence to remember the departed, and that was it.

He still doesn't know if Sally has heard yet, had looked for her after the service, but she wasn't around. Perhaps Munford already told her. He hopes not. He should tell her. He looks over at the telephone. Can't tell her that way. He'll stop by after he finishes his work, perhaps after dinner.

All this is fine, he thinks, scrolling down to the end of the document.

Take as your model the humble sparrow. The sparrow never flies south for the winter. Therefore, it represents the soul of man striving to be at one with God under any conditions. In difficult times—times when the specter of war is constantly looming in the Middle East, when crime rates seem to go up with each passing season, when television and popular music increasingly challenge our sense of decency—God's plan for us is not always obvious.

However, this is also the Sunday before Thanksgiving, a secular holiday, but one which provides an opportunity to reflect on spiritual matters. It's fitting that we take time now to appreciate all of God's gifts to mankind, especially His forgiveness of our sins, past, present and future.

He'd left in the part about the sparrows, despite thinking he should maybe drop it. He'd written a note on a scrap piece of paper, "No sparrows," but he couldn't find the note now. Could maybe take it out of the written version. Kind of a tortured metaphor.

He wonders how many people in town, in his congregation, remember the Dobby of twenty years ago, or a quarter century ago, or recognize whatever it is he became, that splotch on the sidewalk. Surely, a lot of them did. He knew Dobby his whole life. Kindergarten, cub scouts, junior high, high school. They were never close really. Got into a couple of youthful skirmishes over Heaven knows what.

Back in the ancient and idyllic time when they were on the Lyonness High football team together, Dobby was always the wild one, always bragging about how many cans of beer he'd swallowed the night before. He was always surrounded by those two inferior personalities, Kevin and Edwin. Compared to them, Healy supposes Dobby felt like a big man. But his brand of machismo was all talk, what they call overcompensation. At heart, he was really a nervous, shy, scared kid. A mess of a kid. More of a mess of a man. No wonder at all how things turned out.

A wave of heat from the vent beside the desk singes his nostrils. He stands up to take a couple more drags off the cigarette then returns to the desk. He can feel his pants tighten as he recalls Sally being bent over this very desk.

He can't get distracted thinking about that. There's work to finish. He reads over his sermon once again, from beginning to end. Language to him sounds hollow. After making a few more minor edits, he saves the word processing file and closes the program window.

Behind it is a web browser, where he announces his entrance into a virtual room.

Horny Priest: Good evening everyone. Anything to confess?
Devious(F): Forgive me father, for I have sinned. * grin *

Chapter 27

From time to time, vaporous bubbles of conversation, wisps of whispers and discarded monologues escape the conscious universe and sift through the diaphanous haze that covers the realm of the childgod. These dewdrops of interlocution then sit like candy-colored jewels on the inner dome of the childgod's empire until they are licked up by a draconian tongue or picked like nits by simian dolichodactyls.

One such exchange occurs in a Lincoln Towncar among three septuagenarian spinsters, all of them, deaconesses at Incarnation. The three ladies are on their way to plan their annual Christmastime charity drive— Poinsettias for the Shut-ins.

"It is a shame about Johnny Alexander."

"Do you know, I think I taught him in seventh grade? He was a shy boy, but real smart. Creative too."

"It is so sad, isn't it, how some people turn out?"

"Wasn't he married to Owen Herring's daughter?"

"Yes. Divorced years ago though."

"Shush, I think they're talking about it on the radio."

. . . WAS FOUND DEAD IN FRONT OF A CHURCH IN LYONNESS THIS MORNING. MORE ON THAT STORY AT 6 . . .

Nearby at the Kettle diner, proprietor Bull Schuster tears off a check from his pad and places it in front of Stone, who sits across the counter from him. Lucius Gray is behind the kitchen wall with his back turned, scraping the dregs of Stone's home fries in the garbage. Stone, after a long sip of coffee, speaks.

"Did you know him?"

"He was a bum. Literally, a bum. A human waste basket."

"Sure, but did you know him?"

"Who can know these people? You might know who they are, where they came from, but ultimately, they are just scum."

Stone lights a cigarette and motions to Bull for a refill. "He was the patriarch. He fell like Finnegan."

"What's that supposed to mean?"

"Never mind."

Bull continues wiping the counter, then turns and leans in toward Stone as he pours more coffee into Stone's cup.

"People like that are worse than niggers. You know what I saw on the TV yesterday? Apparently, there's a whole country in Africa run entirely by nigger women. Probably ain't a man in the whole place does any work."

"I can't even believe you just said that with Lucius right over there."

"Ah, he's deaf as a bat, and he's knows I'm just kidding anyhow. Ain't that right, Mr. Bojangles? Jigaboo . . . Boogeyman . . . See? No response at all."

Stone fidgets in his seat, takes out his wallet. "Let me ask you something. Why are there so many white people in this town?"

"What do you mean?"

"What if I told you I was black?"

"I'd say that's news to me."

"Well, my grandmother was."

"You're shittin' me . . . Er, but I do apologize if I offended."

"You just don't get it. You're hopeless. This'll cover the check. I'm outta here."

. . . THE INVISIBLE PEOPLE: WHO ARE THE HUNGRY AND HOMELESS IN OUR AREA?   CHARITY RODGERS ANSWERS THIS QUESTION AT 7 . . .

A bell rings for the Reality of Sobriety Group meeting. After the preamble and other formalities, a lanky gray-bearded man in crimson dress shorts and white golf shirt takes the podium. "Hi, I'm Kevin, and I'm a grateful recovering alcoholic."

"Hi Kevin."

"First off, I just want to announce that, in response to a group conscience taken at the last business meeting, we've established a non-smoking area in the meeting room—those three chairs over there that are closest to the door."

There's a smattering of laughter. Kevin grins but retains his composure. After a moment, Kevin's smile flattens out.

"For many alcoholics, myself included, all change meets resistance, even the predictable change of the seasons. It was hot all summer, and I complained about the heat, but when it started to get cool, I got a resentment about that too." Kevin takes a sip of water and waits for this idea to sink in with the crowd. There are general murmurs of agreement. He continues, his face growing more serious. He looks across the room to Sally sitting in the back row, her hands in her lap. "As you all know, we lost someone yesterday, and I'd like to share a little bit about him, and about my history with him. Dobby was a man who grew up here in Lyonness, grew up alongside myself and some of you, and he drank like we all did. He and I and old Edwin Bronson, who also grew up around here, called ourselves the Three Kings of Lyonness High."

He pauses again, breathes deeply, wipes his eyes with a handkerchief, drinks more water. The church janitor, Munford, appears in the doorway, leaning on a broom. After Kevin makes eye contact with him, the sexton disappears again down the hallway.

"Later, I worked with him for a couple of years, installing electric garage doors, and one day, he disappeared. That was about twenty years ago. Then one day last summer, I saw him standing in the middle of St. Andrews Street directing traffic in his underwear. I brought him into this room, gave him some coffee and some clothes, and he came back on several occasions to reach out for help. But he was one of the ones that just couldn't seem to get this program. He was a man with a lot of problems, a lot of mental problems that, compounded with his alcoholism, tortured him his entire life. I'll miss him."

... LATER IN THIS BROADCAST, IS THERE SOMETHING KINKY GOING ON NEXT DOOR? SUBURBAN SWINGERS ...

The Healys' Chinese kids are horsing around in the children's books area, creating a ruckus. but Sally doesn't interfere. She's a librarian, not a baby sitter. No telling where Robbie Healy has gone off to. Kevin Packard sits there reading the paper as he does at promptly 4pm every day the library is open. She's not sure how he manages on Fridays through Sundays when the library is closed. At least he keeps it neatly folded and puts it back where it belongs when he's finished.

There's been talk about acquiring a computer or two with internet service that can be used by the patrons. She's torn about that idea. It's bad enough some of the books they keep around.

Putting the internet in here is probably asking for trouble. But they have to stay relevant to the times.

Her mind wanders to thoughts of Dobby, as it has quite often these last two days. She tries to focus on the good times with Dobby all those eons ago. But most of their time was okay at best—manageable, until it wasn't. There must have been times when they were ecstatic, euphoric with passion. Maybe that first year? It's all a blur to her now.

One of the Chinese girls runs smack into the side of a book shelf, emitting a wail of tears. The Men's room door swings open, and out comes Robbie. He's still tucking in his shirt and has a book tucked under his arm.

"Reverend Healy, you know you can't take library materials into the restroom."

"Settle down Sally. It's a book I brought from home. I had it when I came in."

Seminary in New York City didn't teach that man a lick of couth, she thinks.

❧

To: Ragnell, Victoria
From: Ragnell, Clara
Subj: Things

Glad to hear things are better between you and P. Good luck with the play. I'm sure you'll be brilliant. Nothing much to report on here except the weather. It's been raining for almost two weeks solid, and the lake is flooded. Your father hasn't been able fish, but we're managing with store-bought for now. The rain is welcome, but enough is enough!
Love,
Mom.

॰॰

Monday night at choir practice, Daniel Birch thinks he knows what happened.

Between the understated Youth Choir strains of Jesus Loves Me, he feels a breeze lick his neck. The heat from the building's furnace sharpens his throat. He turns his head and sees the window cracked.

It's a clear cool day, and he stares at the dusk outside, mouthing the words, letting the narrow stream of cold air into his lungs. Beyond his reflection, there is a broad shingled surface. He'd never noticed before, but it looks like you could probably climb right out onto the roof of the Parish Hall from here.

He's been turning the incident over in his mind. His parents never did tell him what they'd been talking about on Sunday after church, but this afternoon he overheard some kids talking about some kind of accident involving a man on the roof of the church. Someone said they don't know what he was doing up there, and they're not really sure how he got up there. He knew that must have been what they didn't want to tell him, and he suspected that the notebooks he found in the basement were connected somehow.

He can see the spot from where he is standing in the choir room, out this window across the garden, the spot where, he imagines, the man must have fallen from. You could get into the basement through that window and then, if you wanted to, and if the yellow door was unlocked, you could make your way upstairs and then up to the choir room. You could get onto the roof of the Parrish Hall from here, and then from there, you could climb right up to the steeple if you wanted to.

Nicole McFadden's is the only single voice discernable over the rest of the choir, a little too proud of her singing lessons, if you ask him. Her mother, Daniel knows, is a piano teacher, and their entire family seems snobbish to him. Daniel has even heard his mother, who very rarely criticizes other families in front of him, has called the McFadden's "uppity."

In his pants pocket, Daniel runs his fingers over the frayed edge of the scrap paper he collected in the basement. Looking out across the gables, it's obvious, there's no way to get up there from outside. But from here, it wouldn't be difficult at all.

. . . MORE CONTROVERSY FOR A LOCAL POLITICIAN. IS AN ALLEGED AFFAIR THE FINAL STRAW FOR MISSISIPI STATE SENATOR EDWIN BRONSON? . . .

At the jingle of the jingle bell hanging from the front door, Ashley straightens from slouching over the front desk at the Sunny Side Up tanning salon.

"Mrs. Birch. It's lovely to see you. Here for the usual?"

"He's having an affair."

"Who?"

"The senator."

"Oh, yeah, him. Speaking of the news, did you hear about what happened at the Episcopal church?"

"Yes, that poor man, Dobby something or other. Did you know him?"

"I don't think so . . . Wait, what did they say his name was?"

Mrs. Birch repeats the name, and it sinks in, hits Ashley harder than she would have expected it to. Patrick's father has always been something of a ghost to Ashley, even when he was still that creepy man who lived in that creepy house around the block from her. He was always in the yard with a bottle and a cigarette and with that auspicious grin of his. Her family didn't drink; they were very religious, and she associated drinking with the devil. So Dobby became for her one of Satan's minions, always lying in wait for her every time she dared herself to bicycle past.

She places Mrs. Birch in her tanning pod.

"Okay, you're all set. I'll come get you in twenty minutes."

She isn't sure if she was yet aware of Patrick back then, although they went to the same elementary school, obviously; there's only the one, unless you travel to another town for private schooling. Only later did she make the father-son connection, and even then, she'd put it all in the back of her mind, never made much of the association. Now, in retrospect, it makes so much damn sense, she wants to cry.

... BRONSON IS SAID TO HAVE HAD A RELATIONSHIP WITH A LOBBYIST NAMED DELORIS STOKES THAT MAY HAVE GONE FROM BACKROOM DEALS TO BEDROOM DEALS. MS. STOKES' RECENT SUICIDE HAS RAISED ADDITIONAL QUESTIONS ...

Rebecca, Dorian, and Karen are snuggled under a blanket on the sofa, watching some fatuous romantic comedy on cable, the way they often like to spend their Sunday afternoons—especially if it's raining, as it is today in Birmingham—when the phone rings. Rebecca, who is in the middle and has control of the remote, pauses the DVR, while Dorian untangles himself and goes to the kitchen to answer.

Rebecca and Karen share a small kiss while, from the kitchen, incredulous interjections then sympathetic epithets filter their way back to the living room. After a few minutes, they hear the faint beep of the hang up, and Dorian comes into the living room looking flush.

"That was my mother. She just told me some remarkable things about Patrick's father."

Dorian summarizes what he knows about it, and, based on the little Rebecca knows about Patrick, it doesn't sound all that strange.

It's a terrible story, of course, a terrible tragedy, but somehow it doesn't surprise her.

. . . BREAKING NEWS. ACCORDING TO LOCAL LAW ENFORCEMENT, SENATOR EDWIN BRONSON OF MISSISSIPPI HAS BEEN APPREHENDED IN PELHAM, ALABAMA AND IS UNDER ARREST. HE IS CURRENTLY BEING HELD AT THE SHELBY COUNTY JAIL IN COLUMBIANA. CHARGES WILL INCLUDE EVASION OF JUSTICE, MONEY LAUNDERING, CORRUPTION, AND POSSIBLY OTHERS PENDING THE DECISION OF A GRAND JURY . . .

The news reporter is just outside Edwin Bronson's holding cell, wearing a baby blue sports jacket and khaki chinos, sporting that preposterous mustache that they all have, talking about the lady lobbyist, Miss Stokes. The Shelby County jail is small but not cramped. Bronson's comfortable enough and resigned to the fact that the end of his reign is coming near. With everything else going on, though, he can't understand why the media is so obsessed with his sex life. He himself can't get his passions up about it nearly as much as these professional talkers do. His brief and unfulfilling affair with Miss Stokes was just another business transaction like everything else. His marriage to the daughter of a senior state senator was yet another, a political marriage if there ever was one. He couldn't even seal the deal by continuing the line. Low sperm count or some such.

The last time he was passionate was right after high school. Sally Herring. That was a long, hot summer if there ever was one, and all the while, they had to hide their affair from Dobby, who was going with Sally at the time, married her shortly after. It was a lovely wedding, in the park. He doesn't think he saw either of them again after that.

. . . NOW BACK TO MORE OF TODAY'S BEST COUNTRY MUSIC ON Z-103. WELCOME BACK FOLKS. I'M JEFF MORGAN, THE BAREFOOT DJ. CLINT AND MARY JANE ARE HERE IN THE STUDIO WITH ME, AND GUESS WHAT? WE'RE ALL BAREFOOT! NOW HERE'S A NEW ONE FROM ONE OF OUR FAVORITE ARTISTS, RANDY TR . . .

Alvin walks into Vanzetti's pizza, places his hands delicately over his ears.

"What on God's forsaken green earth are you listening to and why is it so loud?"

Nick Vanzetti scowls, and turns the radio down to a murmur. "When you take over the shop, you can decide what's on the radio and at what volume. But until then, quit your bitching. Anyway, the news is over. Want a soda?"

"That'd be lovely. Diet if you have it. I have to watch my girlish figure."

For a couple of minutes, Alvin sips his beverage in silence, watching John fill in a crossword puzzle from the morning newspaper. His eye then turns to the white drywall surroundings; it always was empty of décor. A light blue would look nice, maybe some photographs or artwork from local people. The floors are gray tile, bland as can be. A Florentine Terracotta would go a long way toward classing the place up.

"So, Nicola, when's your last day?"

"This is it. I'll come in tomorrow to clean some things out, and tomorrow night I leave for New York."

"We'll miss you around here."

A slow country waltz comes on the radio, and Nick turns the volume up again, and the floor tiles reverberate with the sounds of sad fiddle and steel guitar. Alvin sets his soda can on the counter, and then the two men join hands for one last dance.

☙

To: Ragnell, Victoria
From: Ragnell, Clara
Subj: re: re: Things

The rain finally died down, and you won't believe what washed up from the lake. Dinosaur bones (possibly)! We contacted the natural history museum in Nashville, and they're sending somebody down next week. Very exciting.

Have a good time in Mississippi if you can. Curious to know what P's mother is like.

Love,
Mom.

☙

Now that he's dead, the boy is coming. Sally Alexander neé Herring, as usual, is not dallying. She is vacuuming, dusting, spraying and wiping. She is even baking cookies. She and the boy have never been close—he is a closed-in sort of person, not unlike Dobby—almost alarmingly unsentimental.

Where are they going to sleep? She doesn't know anything about this woman he's bringing with him. A poet or an actress, some such hussy vocation. Well, they're not sharing a bed—not under this roof. It's hard for her to believe he's really not with Ashley anymore, not that they were a perfect match, but they were together for so long. It seems too soon for him to be serious with someone else already. Sally decides to put the girl in Patrick's old room, and Patrick can sleep on the pull-out bed. She removes a folded set of sheets from the hallway closet and places them on the arm of the sofa.

She doesn't really know what went wrong with Ashley, but she certainly understands how things don't always work out.

They had a good life, mostly, for those couple of years, her and Dobby. Sure he had trouble holding a job, and when he drank, he was unpredictable at best, but still they had intimate moments, they had a home, and they were a family. If it hadn't been for the falling asleep in a chair with a beer can in one hand and a lit cigarette in the other, she could have put up with his other nonsense. But they had a child. You can't raise a child in an environment like that. She never thought he'd do it. Never thought he'd make the choice of that life over their life. Their decent life. Then again, she could have a little sense of charity. The man was clearly not in his right mind. It's a disease he had, a disease just like a cancer that slowed his mind and weakened his will.

Briefly, she considers whether she should finally tell Patrick the truth about his father, or what could be the truth, about Edwin Bronson. It had all happened so quickly, and she'd been so scared, and then Dobby was there at the same time, and Edwin was about to go off to law school, and she didn't want to ruin him, with all his potential. She never has been certain about who really was the father, and in many ways, she didn't want to know. Could have been either one. Dobby and Edwin even looked a lot alike in those days. And Dobby was the one planning to stick around, or at least he was at the time, or at least he had no place else to go. Edwin came to their wedding, and that was the last time she saw him. She never said a word to anybody.

The doorbell rings. Beyond the chiffon curtains, she can see Martha Healy waiting patiently, gazing somewhere afar, perhaps at the unfortunate level of vegetation that has accumulated on the roof or at the paint slowly peeling off a window jamb.

"Martha. This is a surprise."

"Yes, well I have something about which I wish to speak with you. It's of a . . . sensitive nature. May I come in?"

"Certainly. Have a seat. Would you like some ice tea?"

"That would be lovely, thank you."

Sally retrieves a pitcher of iced tea from the refrigerator and fills two glasses. While in the kitchen, she removes the cookies from the oven. A little underdone, but they'd be burned by the time she rids herself of this pariah. She sets them atop the oven to cool and then returns to the parlor with the two glasses.

"Now, Martha. What can I do for you?"

"Well, as I said, this is somewhat delicate. But there has been some rumor that the poor man who, you know, passed away near the church last week was some relative of yours."

Her melodramatic tone could not fabricate a thinner veil. Martha's face is awash with anxious curiosity, her unconvincing lips puckered as if to hold in a sadistic chuckle, like a puffer fish just about to inflate.

"Did you really come here to discuss something, or simply to confirm gossip?"

Her features widen, like the beguiling trap of a crocodile's jaws.

"Oh, I'm so sorry to have to bring this up with you, Sally. This really is leading up to something, but I wanted to make sure I have correct information first."

"For Pete's sake, it's no secret. Many, many years ago, in a very different form, he was my husband and the father of my son. We have been divorced for quite some time, more than twenty years."

"I do want to offer my condolences."

"I suppose that's very kind of you Martha, but it isn't necessary. It was twenty years ago when I last knew him, and I'm not certain how well I knew him even then. I barely recognized him when he returned to Lyonness. Now what is this really about?"

"Did he have any other family members in the area?"

"No. His parents passed away many years ago. He has a brother somewhere, but I have no idea if he is dead or alive."

"Considering the circumstances of his passing, the proximity to the church, and the fact that Mr. Alexander was, I suppose, technically, a member of the church, some members of the Episcopal lay council were wondering if the church would have any involvement in the memorial arrangements. Do you know who would be making those arrangements?"

In fact, Sally had spoken to the coroner and taken responsibility for the arrangements herself. Who else would do it? She has to look after him even in death. It's her lot. The body would be cremated. Beyond that, she had made no definite plans yet. Everything the last couple days has been so overwhelming.

"We've considered a small, informal, non-religious memorial service in the park or something. I have to discuss it with the rest of my family, with my son."

"What about the . . . remains?"

"The ashes?"

"Yes, have you considered reserving a spot in the church's memorial garden? The donation requirement is quite reasonable."

Dobby never attended a church service in his adult life, much less paid any tithes, performed any charitable services. He attended the sidewalk breakfasts. That was the extent of his involvement.

"I don't believe I'll be interested in making any donations to the church on Dobby's behalf, but I'll be sure to keep you posted on what we decide."

"Very well then." Martha eyes the sheets folded neatly on the sofa. "Are you expecting company?"

"As a matter of fact, my son Patrick is arriving this afternoon."

"Oh, of course. How nice. How long will he be here?"

"I'm not sure exactly. A few days."

Martha stares in the air again as if her thoughts are a moth flying around the room that she's trying to catch. "Do you think that Patrick might be interested in . . ."

"I very much doubt it."

"I see. No harm in asking. Is he coming alone?"

"I believe he is bringing along his lady friend."

The eyes of the two women dart at each other, heat-seeking missiles sent from opposing forces to obliterate each other. "Oh? Have you met her?"

"No, I have not."

"Well I suppose I should let you get back to what your were doing."

Finally. Sally is quick to show Martha to the door.

"Tell Patrick I said hello."

Were she to actually relay this trite message, Patrick wouldn't even know whom she was talking about.

"I am curious, if you don't mind my asking, Sally—why did you never remarry?"

"I do mind your asking, Martha. Now have a good day."

PART IV: CIRCLES

Chapter 28

The van rumbles down a rural highway somewhere in Georgia en route to Lyonness. The wind whistles in through dry cracks in the weather stripping. In the passenger seat, Victoria dozes with a small pillow between her head and the window. They have a quarter tank of gasoline, which Patrick knows the old vehicle will burn quickly.

A Billy Wayne Carter song comes on the radio, and Patrick turns up the volume so he can hear it above the road noise. Victoria wakes, asks where are we.

"We are somewhere in Georgia."

US 82, also known as the Jefferson Davis Memorial Highway, weaves and turns through State Road 513, US 280, Interstate 20, countless other roads, through countless one-stoplight towns.

"I think we'll be in Alabama soon."

"Patrick?"

"Yes?"

"Are you all right?"

"Yes—wide awake."

"That's good too . . . but I mean with him dying."

"The father? He's nothing to me. I'm going home to help my mother make the arrangements."

"Really? Nothing?"

"Well, maybe that's an exaggeration. But I hardly knew him when he was actively my dad. I certainly didn't know him the way he was when he died. That guy that died was a stranger. Dad died twenty years ago. I've dealt with that. Or, I guess I'm still dealing with it, but anyway I can live with it."

He knows she is thinking that he is holding something back, not expressing his true feelings. The women in his life have often accused him of withholding in this way. The truth is that he doesn't feel anything, and he has nothing left to say. His thoughts are completely drained. He recognizes the stare that indicates that she is trying to read his thoughts, trying to interpret the pain, but there isn't any. He is just numb. He knows she desperately wants to know what's going on inside him, but there is nothing to report. He is not even present in his own mind, a dangerous and haunted world that she wouldn't be so anxious to see if she knew more about it.

One thing he won't say is that he's more worried about seeing his mother, who has always appeared to be without any darkness within her, and that alone makes her seem suspect. It isn't that she is prudish . . . or perhaps she is, but also that she makes herself appear naïve, and it just isn't possible that a person of her experience is naïve in those ways. As far as he knows, she hasn't been with a man since the father, and if she has . . . Well, it's one thing to kiss and tell, and it's quite another to hide your entire life away.

He doesn't want to see her upset. Their relationship has never been sentimental. He and his mother have never really shared their emotions with each other, and he doesn't want to be in a position to have to comfort her. He's not sure how to do that. No doubt Victoria would find this statement alarming were he to speak it out loud.

They need to stop to fuel the van and get a diet soda, his latest addiction. There's an old man in a go-cart doing doughnuts in the middle of the parking lot of the gas station. Perpetual. Patrick wonders how long he's been at that. Difference is, Patrick notes, that we make larger circles. Old man, old man . . .

Pellagra
By Daniel Birch
Forth Grade
Mrs. Gangnagel's class

Pellagra is a disease caused by not eating enough niacin wich is also called Vitamin B. Pellagra is now very rare because many foods are made with extra vitamins. However, in the early 20th Centery, many poor Southerners died from pellagra because they mostly et foods what did not yet contain this vitamin.

The symptoms of pellagra include dermatitis, diarrhea and dementia. My mama, Nancy Birch, says dermititis is like having a rash, and dementia is when you are awake but dreaming. I guess I do not need to mention what diarrhea means.

I am glad that bread and other foods now contain niacin because I do not want these symptoms.

When Patrick and Victoria arrive at his mother's house, Patrick notices that jasmine weeds have taken over the lattice work at the front of the house. He parks his van on the street in front, and then they shuffle up to the front door, bags in hand. The doorbell softly chimes somewhere behind the concrete block wall, and in a few seconds, she's standing there, looking every bit the spinster librarian he always imagines her to be with her red hair up in a bun and those leashed spectacles.

He puts his duffle bag on the ground, and they exchange a brief hug. "Mom, this is Victoria."

"It's a pleasure to meet you Mrs. Alexander."

"Oh, just call me Sally."

His mother, Sally, smiles. He's never in his life considered her a Sally; always just been Mom. They go inside, and he looks at the familiar décor—full of wicker and dried flowers, predominantly blue. In the living room, a glass case displays a collection of tiny chairs. Victoria fawns over them, saying that her father would adore them. Against another wall, a small choir of hand-sewn angel dolls has been piled artfully on a chair. Neither the chairs nor the angels were here the last time he was in this house, which may have been two or three years ago.

She's going to make them sleep in separate rooms, which he finds irritating, but he's not going to put up a fight about it. His mother shows Victoria to the room where she'll be staying, his old room, and he hears her say that she'd like to speak to "her son" privately for a few minutes.

This makes him nervous, especially when he hears the bedroom door close. His mother comes back into the living room, a somber furrow in her brow, and Patrick sits down on the sofa.

"Something's been on my mind, which I think you deserve to know about . . . It's rather difficult, but I've put a lot of thought into how to tell you this. The first thing is that when Dobby and I married, I was already pregnant with you . . ."

"Math was never my best subject, but I figured that out a long time ago . . ."

"Let me finish. I was already pregnant with you, and at that time, before the wedding, Dobby and I were not exactly dating exclusively. In other words, there's a chance, albeit a small . . . ok, maybe a fifty percent chance, that another man is your real father."

He had been wondering why she was saying "Dobby" when she usually refers to him as "your father." All part of the prepared speech. He's so stunned that doesn't know what to say in response at first.

"This other man—do I know him?"

"No. He left town before you were born."

"Well . . . who is he?"

"It's not important. I shouldn't have said anything. I didn't mean to alarm you."

Patrick takes a breath. This news is still hard to take in. For one thing, he can't believe his mother—this woman who never even said 'hell' in front of him—actually had . . . sex . . . with more than one man while she was still a teenager. And the father who he never really knew could be someone he really never knew.

"I'm not alarmed. I'm just . . . shocked. I want to know more. I don't understand who you're protecting by not telling me."

"I haven't spoken to him since before you were born. Anyway . . . There's another thing I need to talk to you about. I should be getting the ashes tomorrow or the next day. Do you want them? "

"Hell no."

⁂

Victoria soaks in the surroundings of Patrick's childhood room. There are no obvious signs that he ever lived in here, although when she opens the closet to put away some hanging clothes, she finds some boxes of comic books and baseball cards among the rolls of Christmas wrapping and other refuse stored away there. The beddings in the room are distinctly feminine, complete with a flower-print duvet and frilly pillow shams.

Needlepoint aphorisms hang on the wall, surrounding her with good advices about motherhood and family. There are some framed photographs of Patrick on the side table. Baby Patrick looks very serious in footed pajamas. Here he is at maybe six, strongly resembling his adult self, in a coon skin cap and carrying what she hopes is a bb gun. She wonders if this family photo is the only one with all three of them. Sally has a tight perm and a pretty smile. Patrick's father is smiling also but the smile seems forced, and that Burt Reynold's mustache isn't doing him any favors either. She sees a bead of sweat just under his hairline. Patrick's face looks most like his mother's in this picture—it's those deep green eyes—though he's clearly not too happy about wearing that yellow suit.

Victoria feels tired after the long journey, so she stretches out on the bed.

A Brief History of the
Lyonness Episcopal Church of the Incarnation

Incarnation is Lyonness's only Episcopal house of worship, with approximately 400 parishioners and room for many more within the elegantly stained-glass decorated, cruciform cathedral. The church is built on two small hills on St. Andrews Street in Lyonness, Mississippi.

The cathedral is at the highest point of the first hill. In the valley, the John Blaylock memorial garden beautifies the front of the building. Behind the garden is the administrative building, which houses the rectory and the church office, as well as the

Parish Hall, used for breakfasts, prayer meetings and other social events at the church. Inside the Parish Hall, there is a thrift store, which splits its proceeds among a number of local charity groups and a small, utile kitchen. The Sunday School Classroom building is built into the side of the other hill, and a playground sits atop the hill, overlooking a wooded area with a creek.

The vestibule contains stained glass portrayals of the saints Mathew, Mark, Luke and John. The stained glass windows on the North wall of the nave depict the Holy Family, the Annunciation, Mary Magdalene with the risen Christ, and Christ at Gethsemene. The South wall contains the Angel at Christ's Tomb, Modonna [sic] and Child, the Good Shepherd, and Jesus in the temple. The West wall holds the largest and most publicly visible window, which depicts the Incarnation, thus the name of the church.

When the church was built, in 1902, Lyonness and the surrounding area boasted a lucrative marble industry. Therefore, marble was used liberally in the construction of the building, including the altar.

Chapter 29

Daniel walks by the church playground on his way home from school. Thinking of the dragon he's still carrying around in his pocket, he wonders if that window to the catacombs is still unlocked. Nobody's around, so he slips behind the bushes. Sure enough, it slides right open. His knees get a little dusty as he crawls through, but otherwise, he easily shimmies onto the bookshelf and then takes a short leap to the floor.

His landing reverberates through the empty halls, so he stands perfectly still for a few moments to see if he hears anyone else. The box is still there in the coat closet; nothing seems to have been moved. He opens a notebook. He can't really read the handwriting, especially with only the small amount of light coming in through the window, and what he can make out doesn't make sense to him. There are more of those doodles spread periodically throughout, sometimes taking up a whole page, sometimes just filling space in a corner or margin.

The overhead lights buzz on, and he knows he's been caught. That church janitor is standing in the doorway, not saying anything, looking disappointed, an unlit cigar dangling from his lip. Daniel rushes to explain himself, saying that he found this stuff on Sunday, and he wanted to take a closer look at it, and he noticed that the latch on this window was broken, and he thinks that the man who fell off the church came in this way and then went upstairs and out through the choir room.

"Go on. Get out of here, and don't let me catch you sneaking around here anymore."

Daniel brushes past the man and up the stairs. The janitor follows him part way, shouting after him.

"You can leave through the back of the Parish Hall. The kitchen door is unlocked."

Now alone in the catacombs, Munford takes a notebook off the top of the stack and begins reading, flipping through the pages. He closes this book and examines the next one in the box. More of the same whatever this is—a diary, a novel, some kind of political treatise—it's all over the place. There are no headings or dates and few paragraph breaks—just variations in ink color and in the legibility of the hand writing. It's one long continuous scroll of near nonsense.

The lettering in the notebooks is tiny and compressed, difficult to read—a script that had to overcome numerous obstacles to get on the page, which according to his assessment may possibly include delirium tremens and fleeting thoughts. The letters slant in all directions, sometimes almost completely sideways, and they contain inner loops so large they seem like letters within letters.

Dees are nearly indistinguishable from ohs, and tees are nearly identical to eyes. The paper is yellowed and reeks of smoke.

He can't believe that ten-year-old figured it out before he did. Some investigative reporter he is, he thinks sarcastically. Well, as much as he always wanted to do investigative work, there wasn't much call for that in Tupelo.

There is a pint of Old Goat bourbon, not quite empty, wedged between the inner wall of the cardboard box and the stack of notebooks. Underneath the notebooks, there is a pair of socks, a light button-down shirt and a black faux fur hat with earflaps. He wonders why Dobby wasn't wearing his hat. It was cold out that day.

Again, he tries to read some pages of the first notebook. Amongst the madman ravings about spacemen, magic monkeys and talking lizards, he occasionally sees some familiar names, names of people in the town. But even the recognizable elements are elusive. There are rather paranoid rants about various people, including Edwin Bronson, who's been in so much trouble lately. What little of it he can understand intrigues him, both as a reporter and as regular person haunted by ghosts of his own.

In the dim, flickering, fluorescent light of the church basement, he can imagine his dead relatives lingering in the walls, their ashes stored just around the corner in the memorial garden. He doesn't usually think of them as being there in the garden, but in his house, always with him, among the ornithology books and photo albums. But in reality, they are right here, just on the other side of this wall.

He decides to take the notebooks home and read them over more carefully in better light, over a glass of bourbon. He fishes in his pocket for a match to re-light his cigar and happens upon the slip of paper that he found on the floor in the hallway upstairs. No sparrows. Why not, he wonders. It must all mean something.

ॐ

The great metallic green box, grinding and growling is the air conditioner, about three feet wide and as tall as the ceiling, and its roar is mighty and loud. Still, the air is stale and hot. This beast, this great machine is all talk. I am the opposite, I think, doing much, saying little. Okay, I'm not really doing that much either. I'm in the King's town, but there ain't any kings around here, alien or otherwise. No lost boys either, just shabby old men like me, talking about football and pussy like they always do, nothing worth noting, but I note it anyhow; it's my calling. I always drink whiskey too fast if I mix it, so I'm having it straight up. A good bartender gives you a glass of water too. According to the teevee, it's dangerous hot in Texas, but here in Memphis, it is merely miserable. I'm sipping, taking my time, if more than a couple go down too quickly, there can be trouble. My name is next on the chalkboard signup for the pooltable. Rack me break me sink me, I'm yours for as long as the fifty cents may last. Call me Q and my partner Old Scratch. To me, this is hilarious, I don't have a partner. I have my usual, sign up for the pool table, and put a dollar in the juke and then I watch a girl, confused over the messy list of names on the chalkboard, trying to clean it up. I see her erasing my name, and I correct her. An honest mistake, but unnerving just the same, to be erased so casually like so much refuse. When I turn back around, there's a woman sitting at the bar wearing nothing but a towel. I overhear her tell someone there was a big fight, I had to get out of the house, it's okay, I'm legitimate. I wonder what that means, legitimate, she seems real enough, flesh and blood, much as any of us, more than some. Last night, the bartender slipped me a free drink. I guess that means I'm a regular now. Perhaps that's what she means, she's a regular. I talked to another woman on another night, and I offered to buy her a beer. She informed me that she doesn't pay for beer here. I said to her you must be special.

Virtually alone in the country patchwork confines of his

mother's house. After their talk, she went over to the library, where she'll be working until evening. He decides not to wake Victoria, who's napping comfortably on his bed. He's hesitant to go out, afraid of whom he might see. Chances are good that he'll see everyone he doesn't want to. But he's both bored and anxious. He feels the eye of the demigods on him, and he knows that the moment has come for him to face their judgment. He hopes it's merciful and swift. Even the clouds outside the window seem to crown the sky with a barrister's wig. He dons his heavy coat and steps outside.

His feet take him across the two-lane highway toward the woods, but the woods, his woods, aren't there. Acres of trees, gone. The land has been cleared and a dinosaur clan of construction machines rest from their labor on a field of red clay. As Patrick gets closer, he can see that a few houses have already been completed down the road—simple one-story structures in the cracker style with large front porches and landscaped shrubbery. A sign on the road leading into the new subdivision labels it "Edwinwood."

"Awful isn't it. The architecture is just pedestrian as can be."

The voice behind him is Zord's. He recognizes the lilt and squeaky timbre right away.

Patrick ignores him. Fuck the architecture. Those were his woods. And Bobby's. The old chicken coop has obviously been reduced to rubble and transported to the nearest landfill. Zord continues.

"Terrible name too. Built from the profits of Senator Bronson's hurricane profiteering, and the egotistical bastard couldn't resist putting his own stamp on it."

Patrick knows this must all be true, based on what he can piece together from the news lately. But so what? These were his woods. He wanders down the newly-paved road, the plots of land stripped to nothing but red clay. He hears Monkeyman whispering behind him. Wind and sweat. Rock and rain. This is not a problem. This is just the beginning of his deserved sentence. So much for that. He turns around and walks in the other direction.

Minutes later, he is in the driveway of his old house, Ashley's house. Now though, he's a stranger here. He wonders for a second whether he should knock, realizes he's forfeited the right not to knock. His other option is to just leave. Before he raises a knuckle, he hears the muffled putter of bare feet on tile, and he knows by the heavy sound that it isn't Ashley who always seems to almost float when she walks.

He shouldn't have come. He's too late. As he turns to walk away, he hears the door open behind him. The clack of the bolt lock echoes in his mind for a moment and then falls away along with his ego. He turns around to see a wet-haired Stone, naked except for a towel, shivering slightly in the doorway.

"Patrick? Oh God."

"Oh God."

"Um, this is awkward, obviously. Ashley isn't here. But, do you want to come in? Maybe we should talk."

Wind and sweat. Rock and rain. He repeats this mantra to himself. Out of a sea of brain noise, Harold's gruff lisp beacons portentously, whatever punishment is rendered meet. That's what he knows awaits him, what he knew was coming when he made the choice to leave, what he knows he has no choice but to accept. But he doesn't have to dwell on it.

"What do we have to talk about? I didn't see anything. I wasn't even here."

"Patrick . . ."

"Look, I'll be in town a few days. Maybe I'll see you later. Maybe we'll talk then. Right now, I can't."

Without waiting for another word from Stone, Patrick retreats down the pothole-pocked road. The demigods now materialize out of the condensation of Patrick's exasperated breath. They stare.

They follow. They remain ominously silent amidst the clamor of peeping chickens and barking dogs. At the end of the block, Patrick begins tearing at his hair, and he addresses them.

"What? What the fuck?"

The demigods say nothing. Monkeyman stares back at him with his usual wide-eyed curiosity, and Harold lingers in the background, detached and almost translucent. Zord is serious and anticipatory.

"Are you going to tell me that she has as much right to happiness as I do, perhaps more of a right? Because, guess what? I know that already."

Monkeyman bares his teeth. With brow furrowed, Zord responds, "Patrick, this isn't some kind of a trick. We're not trying to force you to admit any mistakes or realize any grand truths. The fact of the matter is, there aren't any such things."

"There aren't." He half asks, half agrees.

He's at the dead end street that runs into the back of the church. Monkeyman and Harold are gazing beyond the tree line, where Patrick can just see the top of the steeple. Submitting to an indistinct urge, he jumps the fence, and crosses the church playground with the trio of demigods in tow. He passes the memorial garden and finds himself at the front of the stone building. He can feel in his bones, in the pit of his chest, this is the spot, right in front of the imposing double doors, the spot where the father fell.

He searches deep inside himself for a reaction. It's just a block of concrete, like hundreds of others in this town, like millions of others lining the sidewalks of the world. This slab of cement doesn't tell him anything, doesn't have any answers, certainly doesn't contain the old man's soul.

As he moves on and turns the corner, a short, balding man backs out of the side door of the church, carrying a couple of garbage bags. The demigods float away into the whispering clouds. Instinctively, Patrick tries to hide in the shadows, but after the man drops off the bags and turns around they find each other face to face. He has a stogie clenched in his teeth, unlit.

"You're Sally Alexander's kid?"

"Yes, sir."

"Family resemblance. My condolences on your loss."

"Um, thanks. And you are?"

"Munford Coldwater. I know your mama from her work here at the church. Hey, I've got something for you. Come with me."

Patrick follows him into the church and down a set of stairs, into the catacombs. He attended Sunday school classes down here as a kid. From the coat closet in one of the old classrooms, Munford pulls out a milk crate and hands it over to Patrick. Inside, there are several spiral notebooks. "What is this?"

"Your inheritance. Or at least, I think it rightly belongs to you. Let me know if you find anything interesting in there. I couldn't make heads or tails of it."

Patrick follows Munford back out to the street, meekly thanks him.

"My pleasure. I hope it works out for you. Do you need help carrying that home? I can give you a lift."

"No thanks. It's a short walk. I've got it."

Confused, holding the strange gift, Patrick watches Munford return into the confines of the church. With nothing else in mind to do, and not wanting to carry the crate around any longer than necessary, Patrick returns straight to his mother's house.

Been in the freezing hell they call Minneapolis for a week, doing day labor for drink money, work hard so I can drink in bars, sleep in a heated room, continue my search for the childgod and what he wants with me. Now, I'm at the bar down the way from the SRO where I'm staying. It's early, I spose, only men in the bar. I helped unload a truck this morning

and got a fifty dollar bill, which the bartender reluctantly gives me change for. I consider joking that I will gradually give most of it back over the course of the evening. Instead, though, I just say thanks and let my silence speak whatever it will to him. He is somber, as always, and I feel a bit foolish tonight. I also consider joking that this ain't the bar for picking up women, but instead, I regress to my whiskey and notebook, my darkness, my solitude. Can't explain, Roger Daltrey suddenly screams from the jukebox, a song from my distant and fleeting youth. Feeling good now, yeah, but I can't explain. Yes, it's like that isn't it? The jukebox is the poet tonight. I'm just the transcriber. I don't talk to strangers, generally. I'm a good boy, so they say, a good citizen. That has stuck with me into adulthood, and as I sit at the bar with my usual, my darkness, my solitude, here suddenly is a woman—a gorgeous woman with long, dark hair and a stylish dress, and she sits at the bar next to me. She must be waiting for somebody. Just as I'm thinking, She must be waiting for somebody, there he is—young guy, thin with full lips and perfect teeth. I console myself knowing that they'll both be monkeys soon enough.

When Patrick gets back to his mother's place, Victoria and his mother are sitting in the living room together, both reading—his mother the newspaper and Vic one of her school books. He wonders what's been going on here while he was gone. His mother and Ashley never really got along, but essentially ignored each other. The same thing seems to be happening with Vic. Victoria asks where he's been.

"Just walking around. I ran into a guy from the church, and he gave me these notebooks. I don't really know what they are."

His mother, probably coming to the end of whatever article she was reading, finally looks up from the paper, asks if he ran into anybody else while he was out. He shrugs and sets the box down, scrounges through the sections of the paper his mother has already discarded. Finding nothing interesting enough, he takes a spot on the floor near the end of the sofa and picks a notebook from the top of the stack.

Immediately, he's rapt even though he isn't sure really what he's reading. Gradually, the feeling of vague familiarity turns to recognition. Of course, as Munford said, this is his inheritance. He reads on, utterly fascinated. The notebook is page after page of sheer insanity, but between the lines . . . well, the parallels are unmistakable and, he has to admit to himself, heartbreaking. Dobby even uses that phrase "childgod," a name Dobby had called him on the night before he disappeared, one of the few memories Patrick held onto from the time he spent with Dobby. He scratches his head, puts the notebook down for a few seconds and stares at the ceiling. Maybe he never knew his father, but maybe there's some value in finally getting to know Dobby after all these years of resentment. This is a project he feels he can really sink his teeth into, and he decides that he'll study these notebooks until he knows them cold.

Had to head back down south, back to warmer weather, hitched a ride to Davenport with some travelling musicians who, like me, were lost, lost expletives, they said, whatever that means. They're performing at this bar later tonight. Me, I'll just sit here. They bought me a beer, and it's good, I try to take my time with it. Beer goes down so easy, like nothing. Too much of nothing makes a man feel ill at ease, as a bard once said. They sure do make some noise, these boys, but there seems to be messages in it. A lot of things flashing into my mind from days of yore, homes and folks long ago lost in the waters of oblivion. From behind the bar the childgod in his mysterious wisdom delivers a clearer message to me in the form of a teevee story about the Mississippi congressman named Bronson. The name bounces around in my consciousness for a while. Son of Bron. I know him and he's in trouble. I

feel a deep need in my gut to somehow come to his rescue, but nobody knows where he is, so what can I do? I am only a poet and a drunkard, and I'm a poor poet. There is a connection to New Orleans. City of the Saints. Maybe if I go there I'll pick up more clues. Smoke a cigar like Columbo, ask people random questions.

୬୧

Although the chili with venison smells amazing, Victoria doesn't have any. Patrick neglected to mention her vegetarianism to his mother, so she contents herself with a baked potato and a salad. She'd suspected there wouldn't be a lot of options for her here, foodwise, so she packed a variety of protein bars. Ms. Alexander asks her if the food is okay, her voice revealing her resentment about the refused chili. "It's very good thanks. The chili smells really good. I'd have some except for the fact that I haven't eaten meat in so long, I'm afraid it would make me s . . . I mean disagree with me."

Patrick's mother doesn't answer, still looks annoyed. Fortunately she and Patrick both eat quickly, and dinner is over soon. Victoria eats the last couple bites of her salad and then takes her plate to the sink to rinse it off. Ms. Alexander meets her there.

"If you're not going to eat the skin, give it here. I'll put it in the mulch out back. Don't worry about the dishes. I'll do them when I get home later."

Ms. Alexander has some kind of meeting in the church. She gathers her things and leaves, saying she'll be back in a couple of hours. Patrick immediately returns to his reading on the living room floor. Victoria doesn't think she's ever seen him so absorbed in something. It's refreshing, and it suits him. She sits behind him and rubs his shoulders. He still hasn't said much about the contents of the notebooks, except that they belonged to his father, or Dobby, who may have been his father.

"Anything illuminating in there yet?"

"I haven't really processed it yet, but one thing I'm pretty sure of now; he was my father. These things are as good as a DNA test far as I'm concerned."

"You know, I was surprised you let your mother off the hook so easily about that . . . the paternity question."

"Hell, you know . . . Neither of us likes confrontation."

"I'm sorry, honey. I'm sure this is all much harder on you than you let on."

"No, I'm fine. It's been weird, but my whole life has been weird. I'm kind of used to it."

She knows that just can't be true. He's good at hiding it, playing it down, but she's never met a man with such complex feelings. As much trouble as he's been—to her, to her parents, to himself—she's sure there's a scared little boy hiding in there under all those layers of armor. She slides down onto the floor next to him and gently takes away the notebook, setting it aside as she crawls up onto his lap and kisses him.

"We've got two hours before your mother comes home."

He smiles. She slithers down his torso and unzips his pants.

Chapter 30

Their second day in town, it's sunny out, so Patrick takes Vic to Foley Park. When they get there, he sits on the grass to smoke a cigarette, something that feels to him like an ancient ritual now. Across the lawn, under the great magnolia tree, four women are composed around a blanket with a wicker basket, wine bottles, plastic cups, paper plates. Patrick points them out to Vic, telling her that these ladies have been eating lunch in the park almost every day for years. They overhear the tallest of them declare in a loud nasal voice that she'd been antiquing earlier that morning and passes her find to the others in the group, a silver bowl on a pedestal.

"There's something medieval about it, don't you think?"

"I just love it."

There are some kids kicking a rubber ball around nearby, and it flies right by Vic's head into the bushes. A red-headed boy in a Godzilla tee shirt runs over and apologizes even as he crawls into the shrubbery to retrieve the ball. Victoria says it's okay but suggests that they go over to the swing set on the other side of the park.

There's a lone kid in the swings, a skinny boy of about ten reading a book. Patrick takes the swing next to the kid, and Vic takes the one on Patrick's other side. Patrick doesn't know the boy, but it occurs to him that the kid's parents are probably his age or maybe a couple of years older, so he probably knows them, or used to. He asks the boy what he's reading and is shown the cover—something about ancient Egypt, but it doesn't look like a children's book.

"Pretty sophisticated book for a kid your age. What's your name?"

"Daniel Birch."

Terrence Birch's kid. Terry was a senior when Patrick was a freshman, kind of a local hero, a good football player, went on to play at Alabama, but didn't make it to the pros. The boy has Terrence's face, his freckles, but not his frame. There's no football in this kid's future.

"Oh yeah, I went to high school with your father. My name's Patrick."

Of course, this doesn't appear to surprise the boy. Every adult he meets went to high school with his father. That's the way it is in a small town. The kid doesn't seem to be interested in talking. Victoria pulls on the chain of his swing and rescues him from the conversation.

"Speaking of reading, how's it coming with the mysterious notebooks?"

"I've only had time to read through half of them so far. There are three more. But yeah, it's really something, although I still don't understand a lot of it. It'll keep me busy for while figuring it out."

Though he no longer doubts that he's his father's son, perhaps, he thinks, all fathers—and all mothers, husbands and wives for that matter—are insufficient, in the way that language is insufficient. It signifies a thing in the abstract, but it will never really be that thing. He's his father's son alright, but that doesn't mean that he's destined—or doomed—to the same fate. He can make different choices, and for the first time, he feels motivated.

He realizes he's been looking at the ground, and he turns to look at Victoria. If he could only find it within himself to tell her just how interesting they really are . . . And he realizes that he's going to have to tell her everything, start fresh if she'll still have him. And that will be his trial by fire. If he . . . or rather if the relationship survives that, it can survive anything else he may throw at it. But he can't do it yet. The thought fills him with anxiety.

Suddenly, Daniel pipes in. "Hey, what are these notebooks you're talking about?"

"Nothing that would interest you probably. Some stuff my dad wrote. He was kind of not right in his head."

"Oh."

"You wouldn't know him. He left town before you were born."

"Was he Episcopal?"

Funny question. Patrick realizes that he doesn't even know where the word comes from, so he can't formulate a smart-ass answer. "In a way, I guess. Why?"

Daniel then stands and digs a folded piece of paper out of his pocket, handing it to Patrick. It's a rough drawing, but Patrick recognizes it—not so much in the details as in the intention, the spirit of it.

"You didn't draw this did you?"

"No sir. Found it in the church. Reckon your daddy drew it."

"Yeah, I reckon he did. Can I have this?"

"Sure. I don't know why I was carrying it around."

Patrick shows the drawing to Victoria. She studies it for a

couple of minutes with a quizzical face and then asks Patrick what it means.

"It's something I made up as a kid, and I told my father about it. A giant lizard named Harold. At the time, he kind of represented everything that I was afraid of, although later . . . well, anyway. This is him."

Ever since the hurricane, this ruined city is as desperate as I am. We are a good match. I've been getting a lot of messages but still don't know what to make of them. Spending the night in a jail cell, the television mentioned that Bronson again, and they mentioned Lyonness, the place where we both came from. Maybe everything is going to circle back to there. Then, walking through the French Quarter today I saw a flyer for that rock and roll band, the lost expletives. They'll be at a place called Checkpoint Charlie's, and I'll be there too, just in case I'm needed.

After Patrick and Vic leave the park, she goes back to the house to study. Her finals will be coming up soon after they get back to Florida. But something about this town makes Patrick's feet want to move, so he stays out, keeps walking.

Soon, the sky turns dark. When he feels drops on his head and shoulders, he runs toward the strip mall down the road for shelter. He paces down the sheltered walkway past the fabric store, the Bargain Town, the apothecary. Across the next street is the strip that houses Vanzetti's, but there's an empty shell where the pizza shop used to be. Alvin is hanging around outside anyway as if nothing had changed, his elbow resting on his hip, a cigarette balanced daintily between his fingers.

"Well, long time no see."

"What happened here?"

"The shop is under new management and is undergoing renovations. You just missed Nicky boy. He left town yesterday, off to New York to live with a drag queen he met on the internet."

"Who's the new owner?"

"You're looking at him."

"You?"

"Yes in-fucking-deedy. I had some money put aside from my inheritance, and I finally found something I wanted to spend it on."

"Well, that sure is . . . interesting."

With a sly glance at his watch, Patrick realizes that if Ashley is at work, this is about the time when she would be leaving, and Sunny Side Up is just a couple of doors down. What will he say if he sees her?

Alvin blows an insouciant smoke ring. "You probably didn't even know Nicky was gay. The fact is: he is the queeniest closet queen that I have ever known."

Patrick is starting to get nervous, and the rain is falling harder. "Hey, it was nice talking to you, Alvin, but I have to go."

"A'ight, now. Toodle-oo." Alvin continues down to the laundromat on the corner.

As if on cue, the tip of an umbrella peeks out of the entrance to Sunny Side Up, then dilates and rushes toward Patrick. He has to make himself known to avoid a collision.

"Hey! Whoa!"

On the other side of the umbrella, it's Ashley. Looking very pretty, despite being obviously annoyed to see him. "Shit. I mean, uh, so how are you?"

"I'm hanging in there. What's with you and Stone?"

"He's been a good friend to me."

"Is that right?"

They both stare at each other. Patrick isn't sure why he's

responding this way, challenging her. He can see himself doing it, and it's ridiculous. So much has changed these few months, almost everything, but has he? It's like he's possessed or something. His mind is doing somersaults, trying to break himself out of this spell. Ashley closes her umbrella.

"We're lovers, ok? Is that what you wanted to know? Do you want me to rattle off the many ways in which he is a better lover than you ever were?"

"No, I just . . . didn't know what else to say to you." He stares at his shoes, which are starting to get soaked. With the wind and rain increasing, the concrete awning of the strip mall is doing less and less to keep them dry. "Look, I think it's clear that we've both moved on. I've met somebody also. Can't we be civil?"

Ashley looks away, looks back at him. "Sure. I'm sorry."

"I appreciate you're saying so. I'm sorry too . . . about everything."

She seems to consider whether to accept this larger apology. He wonders what that would mean, for both of them, if any apology can be enough for what he's put her through. Feeling guilty—being self-conscious about feeling guilty—feels alien to him, like a badly made suit. After a moment, Ashley starts to look annoyed at him again.

"So what are you doing here? I mean, I think I know why you're back in town, but is there a reason why you're here, now, at my workplace?"

"Just a coincidence . . . Really. I was out for a walk, and it started to rain. I happened to be nearby."

"Coincidence. Sure. Whatever. Christ. Well, I don't really have anything else to say to you. So if you'll excuse me, I'm going home."

She puts her umbrella back up and rushes through the rain to the little white Sunbird. He watches her pull away, out of the parking lot, down the street, out of sight.

He walks, damn the rain. He feels purified by the heavy weather, letting it saturate his hair and his clothes, letting its heaviness reproach him.

He continues to walk at a quickening pace through the streets of town, trying to cover as much ground as possible, down Main Street and then down the highway, through sludgy back parking lot puddles, through serene residential enclaves. His throat parched, his eyes burning, his back aching, his head pounding, his feet feel as heavy as if they are pulling chains that trap on hooks everything he passes so that he drags behind him all the buildings of downtown, all the trees of the woods, the clouds, the sun, the moon, the stars from the night before. When he breathes, a pungent odor of himself discourages his lungs. Each step becomes harder to pull forward than the one before, and it seems like miles he has walked until finally the weight around his ankles trips him up, into the wet green grass. He lifts his head, lifting the universe.

He sees a bench.

He sits.

Can sitting make a Buddha? In the search for enlightenment, the knight of Christ wanders, but he is too weary to wander. The Buddha sits, but he is too restless to sit. The French philosophers read the German philosophers who read the Greeks who read the world directly, and is anyone enlightened?

He finds himself searching on the ground for whatever shadow of his mind has left behind its original light. The rain stops, and after a few moments of chill, a redemptive blanket of warmth coats him from the silver sky. A gruff voice whispers to him from behind.

"Did you lose something? Did you lose a contact?" A woman in rags. She taps his shoulder. "Is somebody sitting here?"

He turns his head slowly and looks at her. She wears man's shoes, has man's legs. She wears a familiar-looking black fedora with a white band. Her dress fits loosely like a mystic's robe. Beneath the hat, her head is almost completely covered in scarves of many colors, but when she speaks, he can see the wrinkled potato that is her face and the black and yellow void that is her mouth. And he sees her neon blue eyes, and he sees the abyss and the chaos that lie shortly behind them. And he finds himself gripping the park bench, afraid of dropping over some edge.

She spits a brown stream of tobacco juice into a plastic yellow cup. "Is anybody coming?"

Somebody is coming, in a brown El Dorado that's moving really slowly up the street and stops in front of them. It's that old guy from the church, calling from the window. Patrick slowly stands and approaches.

"C'mon, get in the car. You're soaked."

The kid is sitting by the fire, drying out. He didn't want to go back to Sally's house just yet, so he's here, wearing Munford's bathrobe and talking about those notebooks as if they contained the secrets of the universe. Captain Fancy Pants is all over him, but the kid doesn't seem to mind.

"Do you know how amazing it is? No, you couldn't possibly. But let me tell you, it's fucking amazing."

Munford gives him a glass of bourbon, sits at the kitchen table with his own glass, looking at the fireplace. Damn sparrows, he thinks. Still wondering about that. Course, he had a chimney sweep come out. Had to call one in from Tupelo, and the guy couldn't tell him anything. Just one of those things, one of those things that happens.

"Well, I had a feeling you'd find something in there. Glad I could help. So what is it that's so 'fucking amazing' about it?"

"I wouldn't know how to begin to tell you. Did you know him?"

"Not really. I'd seen him around. He was a drunk. He was having a hard time. That's all I knew. I didn't even know about his . . . history with Sally . . . until later."

"Hmm. Well, I tell you what. He had some interesting experiences, even if some of them only happened in his mind."

Munford laughs. "Yeah, sometimes I wonder about my own mind."

"Don't we all?"

When Patrick has warmed up and his clothes are dry, Munford drives him back to Sally's house. It's stopped raining by then, but the roads are glistening and slick. As the sky clears and brightens his path, Munford drives into the sunset. The supermarket on the west side of town has the cheapest cat litter.

Patrick is telling her all these things. It takes a long time, but she's willing to hear him out. He seems to need to talk about it, and it's so rare that he wants to talk about anything. They lie down on the bed facing each other, and Patrick details the way he left Lyonness without warning, without saying anything to anyone, sneaking off in the middle of the night; his brief infatuation with Rebecca, and how he left her also, for no reason, because he's just crazy, and it's plain from reading his father's notebooks that it runs in the family. Victoria keeps trying to interrupt him, but he won't let her, just puts his hand up and says to let him finish, that he has to get all this out. Finally, he takes her hands in his, and he tells her about this other thing, his visions, otherworldly experiences, imaginary conversations. She never heard anything so fucking insane in her fucking life. It does explain a few things though— overheard conversations when he was alone in the bathroom, the mood swings. He's right. He's crazy.

But maybe that's okay. They have drugs for this. They have specialists. He's not going to be like his father, he tells her, and as soon as they get back to Florida, he's going to do something about it, see a shrink or whatever it takes. "I'm not going to be like him because I don't . . . I don't fucking want to drive you away from me."

"Jesus, Patrick. You have to know that this is pretty overwhelming, hearing all of this. Honestly, I don't know what I feel about it. I have to think about it. A lot."

She's never seen him so emotional. It's weird. She hugs him and then turns onto her back facing the ceiling. The pimples and veins in the cracking plaster ceiling strike her as a map, and her eyes follow the lines from one fissure to another, seemingly random, but as Patrick has said to her, all roads go somewhere. Everything eventually seems to point to the center, and at the center there is a globe of light that once in a while flickers, and there's a ceiling fan spinning around it, causing the bulbous light fixture to sway back and forth in a menacing tarantella dance. At any moment, it seems, the entire ceiling could just drop out.

Patrick accompanies his mother to the funeral home to retrieve the cremains. He was awake all night reading the notebooks, and he's sipping a black coffee in the passenger side seat of his mother's car, Victoria in the backseat, half asleep herself.

When they arrive, he and Victoria wait in the car while his mother goes in to conduct the business. Victoria asks if they've decided what to do with them, him, whatever.

"I've decided."

One phrase from the notebooks, repeated often like a mantra, keeps turning over in his mind. "This is the land created by a childgod." That's where Dobby's been living the last twenty years—the land created by a childgod—and that's where he'll be buried.

Shortly, his mother returns holding a polystyrene box, which she hands to him through the window before she gets in the car. Patrick directs her to drive into the new subdivision of Edwinwood, and they pull up to a lot that's been cleared. Only the foundation frame has been built so far. It probably isn't the exact spot, but he figures it's close enough. He hopes that whoever's moving in here isn't afraid of ghosts.

He gets back in the car for the short ride back to his mother's house, the empty box between his knees, the wind from the open window crashing against his face. Demigods circle above as in a cyclone, ever breathless. The eye of the demigods rises until the car is but a toy on a track; the houses and churches and trees of Lyonness shrinking also, fading into a green blur. And then there are only clouds.